Waiting On Life

One Breath

JL Williams

authorHOUSE®

AuthorHouse™
1663 Liberty Drive
Bloomington, IN 47403
www.authorhouse.com
Phone: 1 (800) 839-8640

Published by AuthorHouse 02/27/2020

ISBN: 978-1-7283-4472-0 (sc)
ISBN: 978-1-7283-4471-3 (e)

Library of Congress Control Number: 2020901540

Print information available on the last page.

Cover photo by: JL Williams

This book is printed on acid-free paper.

Contents

Chapter 1

The Valley

Penny, short for Penelope, took a left on Altos Drive. She slowly proceeded through an old California neighborhood, watching for kids. It was a typical South Bay development in Los Altos. The houses were older and smaller, slab houses built in the 1970s. The yards were well manicured with various landscapes. The houses were similar to Penny and her ex-husband's old home, which had a Mediterranean look and feel.

The day was bright and sunny, like most days since she had moved to California. Although she was adept at driving in the rain, bad weather did make it harder to navigate somewhere new. As a realtor in Seattle, it had often been her job to transport clients from one house to another. She had frequently pulled over in the rain to remap to a route with less chance of flooding, although her clients had become increasingly annoyed as their time traveled increased. She missed a lot of things about Seattle, the inclement weather was not one of them.

She was not sure when the wide street of residential homes would yield to an office building or a commercially zoned residence, but the navigation system pointed her onward a few hundred yards and then to her left. She finally pulled into a narrow parking lot with few available spaces, parking between two gray Priuses. The Prius to her right had new tags, and the one to her left was beat up with a dented bumper. With a few scratches, her own three-year-old Prius was a happy medium.

What are the chances? Penny wondered. She chuckled to herself. *Pretty good in old California.* She eyed the building and located her suite, 1B, wedged between the offices of an orthodontist and a pediatrician.

Penny looked at her watch. She was ten minutes early, which did not bother her. She pulled up his profile again on her phone, but it was a blank page. *Oh well,* she thought. *I might as well go in and see if I can reload his page when I'm sitting in his waiting room.* She hoped to get a better signal, though she was dubious about that.

Penny approached the door and looked up at the number once again, 1B. She had a good feeling as she opened the door and walked over the threshold.

Dr. Hempstead, on the other side of the door, immediately greeted her warmly. "How do you do, Penelope?" he asked, shaking her hand and pulling her in at the same time. He placed his other hand on her arm.

Penny felt as if he were trying to read her in some fashion, which made her uneasy. *No one should be that friendly,* she thought. Still, she didn't have a bad feeling about him as an extrovert or someone who tried to read a new patient's mojo or vibe. Penny had been to a few counselors, starting when she was a teen and ending with a marriage counselor. They all were different in style, but helpful.

But why had he addressed her as Penelope? She had

specifically noted on her profile information request form that she was to be called Penny. She could see that Dr. Hempstead was older, somewhere between eighty and ninety, so she decided not to make waves by correcting him. No one ever called her Penelope, but he might have some fond former attachment to her name, so she'd let it persist. She only hoped it wasn't the same attachment her parents had when they named her after a cartoon character, Penelope Pitstop. Penny had seen the cartoon only a couple of times, but Pitstop had registered with her as silly, backward, and not someone to whom she could relate.

"I do just fine, Dr. Hempstead," she replied. "You were recommended by Ms. Magford, a dear friend of mine who has passed. She said that you were friends for a while and that I needed to come and see you. Ms. Magford was a good friend, and I was lucky to have someone of such grace and wisdom in my life for the time that God permitted. She and I shared a belief in God, and I even attended a couple of her Bible studies, on Romans and John. I'm not sure about your own religious affiliations, if any, but I hope that's not a problem."

Dr. Hempstead smiled and said, "I find it is only a problem or baffling when people deny God's existence. As for Ms. Magford …" He briefly seemed at a loss for words, and then his expression changed to one of joy. "Ah yes, she was a wonderful woman. I quite believe she directed you to me for a reason. Do you agree?" He paused again, although the question was both rhetorical and a personal reflection, before continuing, "Well, let's begin. I don't want to waste any more of your valuable time today." Letting go of Penny's hand and arm, he directed her to the couch.

Penny looked at the brown leather sofa, unable to decide if it was old or new. It reminded her of the couch that used to be in her dad's library. Also reminiscent of her father's library was the much-loved smell of cigars and musty old books that permeated the doctor's office. She recollected how she and her father used to sit together and read. When she was younger, he read to her, but eventually they sat at opposite ends of the couch and read together. Finally, as his eyes started to deteriorate and his mind wandered, she would read to him. She picked up the plaid pillow from the corner of Dr. Hempstead's couch and sat down, placing it beside her.

Dr. Hempstead took up his tablet, and the session began.

Penny asked boldly, "Do you want to talk about my first dream?" She looked at Dr. Hempstead as if he were invisible, staring right through him as she recollected her dreams, her current situation, and how they might be related. She hoped he could be her interpreter.

Penny thought about her dear, deceased friend Maggie. Not much younger than Dr. Hempstead, Ms. Magford had passed away a year and a half ago with her husband by her side. But before she died, she had recommended that Penny see the doctor, whom she had considered a friend.

Penny had not heeded much of Maggie's sage advice until she was in the thick of things with her husband, Rick. Headed for divorce, Penny and Rick had finally sought out marital counseling. Although she had always stood by her spouse respectfully, Penny had not realized the degree of perseverance, honor, and love that marriage requires. She and her husband had been so busy with their own lives that somehow they had drifted apart until eventually a vast ocean separated them. Making time for each other had been at the top of Ms. Maggie's "must do" list, right under praying together and having fellowship and accountability in church.

They had often talked over a cup of tea and biscuits. In the comfort of Ms. Magford's ten-by-twelve kitchen, they had sat and discussed many of life's matters, not just marriage. As a realtor, Penny had noticed that the kitchen was dated. The glossy yellow appliances had been from the seventies, as was the gold-striped wallpaper on an accent wall leading to the living room and the plain, off-white laminate flooring. The decor had pulled her back into decades past.

Other parts of the house had been updated, or at least somewhat renovated within the previous decade, but not every room. It was not in her house, however, but in her garden that Ms. Magford had been most pleased with her efforts. She and Penny would often walk, talk, and sometimes sit as the older woman would tend to her plants. The timeless garden had been always blossoming. Maggie had many prized plants, some of which had even bloomed at night. Penny had often thought it was magical.

Penny had tried to be patient and not impulsive with her elderly friend. She had often prodded Maggie to update her kitchen and had asked if it would be acceptable if she helped in renovating a little bit of the house, especially the kitchen. But Maggie had said that she and Clifford liked it the way it was. Penny had offered to help with costs if that was part of it, but Maggie had said it wasn't. When Penny had asked if changes could be made in the future, the older woman had just shrugged. That had let Penny know that she could bring up the topic in the future, which she did. She could only guess that Maggie and Clifford had saved their time for the things they liked most, such as traveling to see their grandchildren or entertaining their many friends and family.

Penny did not fully appreciate their time together until after Ms. Magford's passing. She could now recall from their conversations and her friend's stories how content the Magfords had been in their home and lives. Penny had felt a sense of love as soon as the front door had opened and a sense of renewal when she left their home. It was in that throwback kitchen that she had gleaned from Maggie everything she needed for a happy life, though she hadn't known it at the time. They had talked about everything that crept into their minds and hearts. Their topics of conversation had ranged from handed-down recipes and the week's weather forecast to conventional wisdom—and even Penny's bewildering dreams.

As they had quaintly sat together giggling, talking, and sipping their tea while eating biscuits, Ms. Magford had told her about Dr. Hempstead, who not only interpreted dreams but was also licensed to counsel those in need. Now Penny could only hope that Maggie's friend and doctor would be able to help her now and make sense of what was in her head.

Dr. Hempstead told her that he'd be able to help her in due time. "I need to get some background information first. You've already told me that your husband issued you a certificate of divorce six months ago and that your father died in his sleep four years ago. Also that you're not going back to live with your family because you don't get along with your mother—the two of you no longer see eye to eye." He looked up at Penny, then back down at his scribble, and asked, "Is there anything on which you want to elaborate?" After a silent pause, he continued, "You also have a sister and a brother to whom you do not speak." Again he looked up at her and then back down at his notepad.

Penny nodded in agreement, though she thought the semantics of these details were a little off. *Who says "issued a certificate of divorce"?* she wondered, but then put it off to old age. "I hope you don't judge me. None of this is my fault. I know I'm not perfect, but I don't feel that I deserve the cards that I've been dealt," said Penny, looking at the ground as her chin dropped. "I've always been a good person, trying to do my best in this life for myself and others. Yet here I am with nothing but bad luck. Not that I feel sorry for myself, because I don't. I know much better people than myself who have suffered through much worse than this. I'm just not sure what to make of where I am in life and how to go forward in the most positive and effective way. I'm open to guidance and a paradigm shift—if you'll pardon the cliché—because I'm a ship without a rudder and headed for the rocks." By now, Penny felt worse about herself than when she had first come into the office.

Dr. Hempstead said, "There is no judgment here. Only One can judge, and there is grace. There is no need to feel bad about yourself or your situation. That's why you're here, in hope of securing an anchor and perhaps a rudder too!"

It seemed to Penny that Dr. Hempstead's last statement might have been an attempt at humor. She smiled at his suggestion of an anchor, and then looking up through tear-filled, beautiful blue eyes, she said, "That would be nice, so very nice." As they talked about her family situation, some of her feelings of guilt were alleviated and she began to feel hopeful. She was at home and comfortable in her surroundings, and the time passed quickly. As their ninety-minute session came to a close, Dr. Hempstead stood up, as he did with all his patients, and extended his hand.

Penny took his hand and was gently helped off the couch. They walked to the door, and Dr. Hempstead put his hand on her shoulder. He whispered, "Things will get better." Awakened, she shrugged his hand off and tensed up as he excused himself. How could he know whether things would get better? It seemed like her life was a culmination of things only getting worse. What would change? After all, life happens to everyone, not just one person in particular.

She looked back at the calm, serene setting of his office, where everything oozed peace and harmony. *How unrealistic*, she thought. *Even the placement of the furniture has balance.* Although there was no waterfall or other central water piece, the surroundings had a sort of feng shui. The pictures hanging on the walls were large and scenic—framed still-life pictures of beaches, meadows, and calm waters. These peaceful images were some of her favorite things, yet they struck a discordant note. She felt uneasy as Dr. Hempstead approached her with a small framed picture in his hand. She glanced at the picture and then looked into his eyes in search for the truth, but he didn't flinch or turn away from the doubt that he saw in her eyes.

Penny wondered about his words, "Things will get better." What change would alter her universe? Things getting better would require change—but who, what, where, why, and most importantly when? She was desperate for answers. Could there have been some hidden judgment for which she was being held accountable? Was her life payback for some past wrong? Maybe she had done something that in some cosmic way had negatively affected both herself and others. Maybe she carried around bad luck that had been passed down through generations. Would Dr. Hempstead be able to help her with that type of karma? Her thoughts could have trailed off on even worse tangents, but she caught herself.

"We don't know that, do we? That things will get better?" she asked Dr. Hempstead, glancing back over her shoulder at him and reaching for the door.

Dr. Hempstead pulled the door open from the top, as Penny turned the doorknob to the right. "Actually we *do* know that," he said. "Things may get worse before they get better, but you will get better. Not that you're ill, although your thoughts do seem to take you to some strange places. There's a grander plan, and we're part of it. We're not just caught up in happenstance, and our thoughts should not blow us about like a ship on the ocean. We should know what we believe and stick to it, but also we should believe in the truth so we can solidly go forward with an anchor point." He paused and then added, "That was a mouthful. I didn't mean to ramble on. Did that make sense, or did I say too much?" Dr. Hempstead prided himself on being a good listener.

He handed her the picture, and Penny looked it over. It was a beautiful landscape with the word *Courage* written in front of a valley. There was also a reference to John 16:33 underneath. Although she had studied the Gospel according to John in a Bible study previously, she wasn't familiar with that particular verse, but she resolved to look it up soon. She was not eager to search through the Bible to find that one verse, but she was thorough enough that she wouldn't let it go too long. She needed to know what manner of *courage* was referenced. Perhaps her Bible would have a footnote that would provide additional insight.

Once again a peace flowed through her, and she realized that her thoughts had become a bit derailed with negative energy and bad karma. The negativity did not coincide with what they had talked about in their session, but courage did. *Courage*, Penny thought.

"Thank you for this," she said. "Also I like what you said about there being a grander design or plan, that we are part of something bigger. Is that what you meant?" She realized she was edging in on some additional time, but she wasn't concerned since nobody was waiting.

Dr. Hempstead's eyes came alive again, as they had in their session. "A bigger plan indeed, designed for Him and you, and tailored for a good purpose for which you are well suited," he said. "Now run along, and think on things that are true and worthwhile. Try not to think about anything that is suppositional or convoluted. Just think about what is pure and holy."

Penny knew that she was outmatched by his candor and confidence. She wanted to say something forceful and persuasive—be a devil's advocate, so to speak—but she was silenced. She had no idea if what he was saying was true, but for the time being she would put her doubt aside. She didn't feel like she was being pushed away, although she was being told to leave. She looked back at Dr. Hempstead as she walked away from his office and nodded okay.

She understood that Dr. Hempstead wanted her to go and be better, but as she left, she began to cry. She had carried so much weight for so long, and now she was just being real, not negative. But a certain comforting peace stayed with her, a hope that her circumstances would not prevail and, most of all, that a guiding force held her in check. As she walked from Dr. Hempstead's office to her car, she went over their conversation in her head and decided to make notes on everything when she arrived at home. She wished she had paid closer attention to his words, but she was surprised that some of them were still with her, especially since their time together had passed so quickly.

Penny got into her car and backed up. Suddenly she heard a deep car horn blow, and she stopped quickly as a black Tahoe whizzed by behind her. A front window was rolled down and the front-seat passenger yelled some choice words about not paying attention, but that didn't bother Penny in the least. She was so happy just to feel some relief from her numbness that she had decided to just feel good for the time being.

Chapter 2

The Betrayal: Best Friends

> Guard your heart more than anything else, because the source of your life flows from it.
>
> —Proverbs 4:23

For the next two weeks, Penny went about her business trying to think positively. She focused on the good and eliminated the negative. She thought how elementary, futile, and primitive her efforts were. But no matter how positive she tried to be, she knew that it didn't really matter in the long run. Hope was fleeting, and so was the truth. She no longer believed in true love, and her hopes for a better life and greater purpose had dwindled to small crumbs by the time her next appointment with Dr. Hempstead rolled around.

Penny was now on the offensive. A brain-dead person had a better chance at happiness than the vast number of people chained to a lifetime of poor choices, regret, failed relationships, and doomed prospects. Life realities were more than fantasy, and truth was relative at best.

Just as Penny reached for the doorknob, Dr. Hempstead walked up behind her, interrupted her thoughts, and asked if he could be of assistance. Then he inserted his key into the door, opened it for her, and said, "Be my guest."

She stepped into his office, smiling faintly and trying hard not to feel comfortable. She had overthought the feelings of safety and comfort at their previous session. Those feelings were not real, she told herself, and she now intended to end her sessions with Dr. Hempstead. Ms. Magford had given Penny sage advice, including coming to see the dear doctor, but that advice no longer suited Penny's circumstances. Her marriage had ended, and she was on her own with only regrets.

Penny politely took a spot in the center of the couch. She didn't reach for a pillow, but sat forward with both feet flat on the ground and her hands in a triangle between her legs. Dr. Hempstead knew immediately that this was Penny's farewell pose.

Penny began slowly, "Dr. Hempstead, thank you for everything, but this isn't going to work for me. I had a hard time digesting everything we talked about in our last session. Although I appreciate the time we've spent together, this type of therapy is not for me. You can charge me for the full session if you'd like, but I have to go." Then she resolutely pulled the picture out of her purse, looked at it with contempt, stood up, and politely held it out for him to take.

Penny was not prepared for what came next. Dr. Hempstead motioned for her to sit back down, and his eyes filled with tears. *No way*, she thought. *Oh, I've blown it. My name, Penelope, must be a connection to someone in his past.* She hated making anyone feel bad, especially an elderly gentleman who had been nothing but insightful, compassionate, and kind. *Well, it cannot be helped*, she told herself. *I'm not responsible for this. He needs to be more professional. Dear God, why tears?*

Dr. Hempstead said, "Of course, it's your choice to have assistance from me or not, but may I suggest that we just finish this session? And perhaps if you choose to stick with our therapy, we should switch to weekly sessions rather than biweekly. Take heed, because this point in your life could be pivotal in your pursuit of happiness. This type of therapy is geared toward results—it's not just about making you feel good for the moment. This therapy involves a specific number of sessions or length of time within which we work." He paused and waited for Penny to acknowledge his statement. "Did you know that?" he asked.

Penny's mind was elsewhere, and she still felt guilty for making him feel bad. She looked at him innocently and said, "No, I didn't know that." Then she quickly added, "There's a specific duration," to indicate that she was at least partially listening, although she was still thinking about his tear-filled eyes.

"Did you not read my profile page?" Dr. Hempstead asked, leaning forward. "You can do this. It's not about positivity as much as roots. It's cognitive, not behavioral desensitizing nonsense, although we have borrowed the end approach from the type of therapy that includes an endpoint. Get it? We will get you to a place where you are better equipped to deal with life circumstances. But make no mistake—it's about you, not about your happenstances."

Penny started to speak and then stopped, not knowing what to say. Then she opened her mouth again, but was still at a loss for words. Finally, out of sheer habit, she said, "Yes, I agree. You can continue to speak." She wasn't sure why she had said that or with which part of his monologue she was in agreement. Nor did she know why he would need her permission to continue. She supposed she just wanted to be in control, but in reality she was only anxious.

Looking a bit puzzled, Dr. Hempstead continued. "We're a function of grace, not perfection. Life isn't perfect, but like Pandora's box, there is hope—and that hope is grace. None of us are here forever. We all exist temporarily in a fallen world where our situations are not ideal and neither are we, no matter how much we try to make improvements. Grace is true and it covers us all if we choose to accept it, but what you make of it is up to you." His eyes were now dry, and his ancient smile graced his face once again.

Penny could not believe she had made him cry. Her eyes were large with bewilderment. Why had he been about to cry? She caught a little bit of what he was saying, but not all of it. Did the compassion she saw in his eyes result from the fact that he secretly knew her? Had he perhaps been a friend of her father's?

Maybe Maggie had told him more about Penny than she had let on? No, Maggie would not have done that, and it was such a long time ago. Also, Dr. Hempstead had not revealed that he and Maggie had been friends when Penny had first brought her name up in their first session. She looked again at him incredulously. *He really should be more professional*, she thought.

Penny did not want to be caught off guard again, although she obviously was. Her posture straightened, and she placed her hands on her thighs. "Okay, I will continue our sessions. I'm not sure how this is going to go, but I'll trust you in the short term." *It will be like trying on a new hat*, she thought. "I'll reload your profile page and look again at the therapy options. I'm sorry I missed that." She looked at the picture still in her hand, put it back into her purse, and smiled back at him.

Dr. Hempstead picked up his iPad and looked at Penny. She nodded for him to continue, but then he put his iPad back down. "What if we just walk and talk?" he asked. "There's a park not too far from here, across the street and perpendicular to the road you drove on to get here. I'll try to keep up with you as we walk. What do you think?"

Penny much preferred to walk than to sit in the comfort of his office, so she readily agreed. They left the office, took deep breaths, and found the air to be crisp and refreshing. A strong breeze tousled Penny's hair, blowing it in all directions. She quickly grabbed it with one hand and pulled a scrunchie out of her pocket with the other. She twisted the scrunchie over her handful of hair and tossed the ponytail behind her. Her spirit lifted, she was ready for their walk to the park with the sun on her back.

They started out slowly. Penny guessed they were walking about a twenty-minute mile, super slow. She looked at her watch to assess her pace and keep track of her speed and heart rate. Conscious of walking too fast, she slowed her pace for the sake of the good doctor, who had jovially mentioned that he would try to keep up. Although he seemed to be in reasonably good shape for being so senior, it was better to play it safe. She did not want another reason to feel bad for him.

Penny, by nature, was a very fast walker. She used to walk quite a lot with some of her girlfriends in Seattle, and they often had asked her to slow down. So she would try to walk slower, but she knew that if she started to talk, her speed would gradually pick up. Maybe she would let the doctor do most of the talking.

As they strolled casually toward the park, Penny decided to go to her constantly nagging question—her real reason for continuing counseling. "So can we talk about my dreams while we walk?" she asked. In her gut, she felt like someone was trying to tell her something through her dreams, but they did not make sense to her. One thought was that an outside force was trying to communicate to her about her future or warn her of something from her past, but she could never be sure. All her dreams were so cryptic, filled with men and women whom she had never met.

Dr. Hempstead acknowledged the need to talk about her dreams, but he told her it would be better to wait until they were more familiar.

Penny did not have a lot of patience and wondered who had put him in charge. He should be at her service, since she was the client. They should be able to talk about whatever she wanted, whenever she wanted. She was not used to being told that she needed to wait for anything. There were other things about Dr. Hempstead's approach that made her uneasy. She was uncomfortable with his personality, which she found to be authoritarian, far too hopeful, and unrealistic.

She would endure it for now, since she needed the help he promised and, most importantly, his interpretation of her dreams. That was reason enough to continue their sessions. She wondered, *What if he's a con or a fraud?* At least he seemed to think he could translate her dreams, and there was the idea of an ultimate schedule for their therapy. That did not hurt her head. Although she had been on the fence about whether to continue their sessions, she found herself swayed toward the positive potential benefits.

She really had nothing to lose and everything to gain. It could go either of two ways, she thought, both of which were acceptable to her despite her immediate discomfort. He could be true to his call and keep to the schedule of just a few months, helping her shift to good karma and shedding some light on her dreams. Or their sessions would end whenever she chose with no upswing for which she would have to mentally prepare. Either way, she was in control.

There also was no negative financial effect of continuing the sessions since most of them were covered by insurance with a ten-dollar copay that was within her budget. She would see it through as long as she could remain patient with the false notion that everything was golden, despite the fact that nothing worked out in her life as she anticipated.

Penny knew that if she thought too long or hard about her current life, she would become depressed, but the obvious was hard to avoid or deny. She had little to no support from her estranged family or her ex-husband. She and Rick had started out as best friends, and they had promised each other when they broke up that they would still be there for each other—no matter what. They had not pinky sworn, but they'd shared a good laugh and cried over a bottle of wine together on a couple of occasions. She would keep up her part of the bargain as she tried to stay true to her commitments.

Penny and Rick had talked about what would happen when they started dating other people and whether that would change their relationship. They had agreed that they would stay friends, although she knew that was an impossible proposition. Their friendship had been the reason they married in the first place, but she wanted to believe they could sustain it. She was tempted to think of herself as a fool and an idiot, but instead she told herself that she was a romantic who did not want her marriage to end.

Penny continued with that train of thought. She had no children, no father, no husband, and only a little savings in her bank account for emergencies. Nothing in her life was upgraded, including her hairstyle, clothes, car, and house, but she managed okay. She would take inventory of her life later when she did not have to keep up her guard for the sake of mental stability.

They crossed a street and headed into a park only a few hundred yards from Dr. Hempstead's office. Penny thought of his age and suggested that he might want to sit for a while, but Dr. Hempstead adamantly refused the offer. He wanted to continue to walk and talk along the paved pathway that circled the park, which was filled with beautiful trees of all types, including cedars, acacias, myrtles, cypresses, pines, and olive trees. He seemed to walk more slowly as he admired his surroundings.

Dr. Hempstead was particularly fond of the pink and white crepe myrtles that bordered the beginning of the pathway and the oak and sycamore trees within the park that provided the most shade. In the center of the park were the largest trees, most of which were redwoods, surrounded by freshly mowed green grass. Picnickers ate and drank under the shade of these large tree while children frolicked and played. Dr. Hempstead told Penny the names and origins of a variety of trees and flowering plants—information that most people would not have known.

Penny did not mind listening to the good doctor, because it reminded her of time she had spent with her father. Her father would point out the differences in the plants on their walks and in their garden. It also reminded her of the time they spent together on their back porch looking up at the stars. On a clear night, under the canopy of night sky, her father would recite the names of the various constellations. They were both fascinated by the infinite possibilities of space, and they had hoped to see the northern lights, which reminded Penny's father of the creation of Earth. He had explained that the shades of red, yellow, green, blue, and violet were the result of gaseous particles in the atmosphere colliding with charged particles released from the sun's atmosphere. Seeing the northern lights together could have been a bucket list item for him, and Penny wished that she had made the time. Now it was her turn to cry, but she didn't.

Looking around, Penny now was in a more sullen mood. She was reminded of why she had moved back to and loved Northern California. She loved its clear skies, big moons, ample sunny days, rocky beaches, pleasant parks, and grand trees. Northern California made her think thoughts of splendor and grandeur combined.

Smiling, Dr. Hempstead said, "It is a great design, isn't it? God did all of this for us."

She looked at him and laughed, thinking how peculiar he was, but he just continued to smile as his eyes soaked in his surroundings. She wanted to walk arm in arm with him, but she was still too angry.

The betrayal of her life thus far loomed in her thoughts and heart. Somehow luckily she was able to blame it on Dr. Hempstead. Otherwise she would have to take account for her lackluster life and own insignificance. Better that it was his fault than hers, as a result of some action she had taken to deserve such a fate. How much more sad she would be to think not that life that happened to her, but rather that she was a flawed, inept person who could not handle her own shit. Things happen, and she had to wade through whatever was put in front of her. This was her life.

Penny looked again at Dr. Hempstead, who embraced life and nature and seemed to see life as an open canvas with possibilities, respect, and goodness. How could his wise eyes not see it, the futility of life in general? Did he not know the torment, persecution, evil, or despair of life? Did he not keep up on current events? If only she could be so ignorant. How could he hold true to his philosophy of courage, perseverance, and positivity? If that is what he truly believed, he was certainly lacking experience, although he most likely was in his nineties. Penny moved a bit farther from him.

As she and Dr. Hempstead looked at each other, she said, "I just don't see how you expect me to have courage when everything in my life is wrong. I am a goddess, and yet nothing adores me. I am alone, and I will die alone. What is the point of having courage?"

Dr. Hempstead did not attempt to placate her, and he had no rebuttal for Penny. Instead, he laughed and asked, "A goddess? Why do you say that?"

Penny's cheeks were flushed. "Aren't we children of God? Aren't we made in His likeness? We are kings and queens, and yet we are fallen. So maybe I'm a demigod or diva who can never rise to the top." She was not proud of her words, which were merely catalysts for her feelings. Unable to look him in the eyes, she turned away, pretending to admire her surroundings. Like a young child throwing a tantrum, she felt herself becoming more agitated with the dear doctor.

Dr. Hempstead continued to watch the birds flutter here and there. He listened to their songs as they softly tweeted out tunes that no one could decipher, but that were pleasing to the ear. Out of all creation—heaven and earth, sky and water, sun and moon, trees, plants, and animals—he most loved people. Penny was especially important to him. Even with all her inconsistencies and vague notions of what to adhere to and what to dismiss, he preferred her questionable company to being alone on this beautiful afternoon. After all, that's why he was there. Dr. Hempstead knew he was the object of Penny's discontent. He was not good at dodging verbal blows, but he was better at taking a hit to the target he wore around his neck.

Briefly stopping, Dr. Hempstead began to speak slowly, revealing that he knew biblical scripture well. "We are created in God's likeness. Genesis 1:27 says, 'God created man in His own image, in the image of God He created him; male and female He created them.' But you are not equal to God, not even by half. The idea that you are worthy of being adored by others and that you are of great importance is a fallacy that you should not entertain."

Penny crimson cheeks became less red than pink, for she understood his reproof. "Yeah, I guess I am not very humble. I am more of a maverick than a diva. I want so much, but I'm not sure what I am entitled to as it equates to goodness. Don't we all have an inherent right to the pursuit of happiness despite our shortcomings? Although I am not sure what mine are," she added. She knew the good doctor's knowledge was vast, but she was not sure how far they could tread without him becoming impatient with her.

Dr. Hempstead offered his arm, which Penny took without thinking. "Sure, we can choose our pursuit of happiness," he replied, "but our choices are not without consequences. As children, we can choose to eat only cake and drink only milk, if it weren't for our parents' direction. And we know that as we grow older, some of our choices can be darker and ill-begotten if not curtailed. So our choices lack nutrition and substance as they reflect on our lives. Knowing good choices from bad ones starts with our fear of God. Do you believe that?"

Penny did not answer immediately. She thought about what the good doctor meant by the fear of God, perhaps an ultimate source of goodness by which to govern our conscience. "If there is no way of knowing good from bad, then any choice can be good—which we know is not true, especially in the case of eating only cake. Is that what you mean?" she asked.

The good doctor nodded. "So do you know that to be a truth?" he asked again. Penny's pace picked up, and he followed suit.

Penny agreed, except for his assertion that knowledge starts with our fear and reverence of God. Which God was he referring to for ultimate, governing goodness? She considered herself a Christian, and she knew that he spoke of Jehovah, the Judean/Christian God. Dr. Hempstead spoke of a holy God who encompasses both good and evil, the only God who could judge between them. Jehovah is the only God who can account for both good and evil and by whom a person can be reconciled to God regardless of who they are, what they have done, their background or earthly origin. The Son of God died for all. Accept that, and you are saved by grace. She knew the creed and believed it within her heart, but still she questioned. The knowledge starts with respecting and acknowledging that there is a God? That was a question for the atheist, and she would save it for a rainy day. She decided not to say anything more on the topic.

Penny leaned a little closer to Dr. Hempstead and whispered. "I believe I have made right choices, especially in God's eyes. I loved only one person and gave myself to him. I vowed to stay with him for all of my life, and that was my intention, but now I am alone. We are no longer best friends, and 'till death do us part' grieves me. I don't mean to be so hardheaded, but I am having a hard time seeing why cake is so bad, since solid food has left me wanting only cake." She once again wished she had not taken hold of his arm, but she continued their stroll arm in arm out of respect for him.

A gust of wind carrying the scent of juniper came and went, and Dr. Hempstead was reminded that he was not alone. "Faith is good. We don't see the outcome of eating only cake as children, but parents do. We are created in God's likeness, and we are His workmanship. He knows the outcome of our choices, good and bad. We should respect Him as God if He is absolutely holy. How can there be any delineation between good and bad if there is not a true dichotomy between right and wrong choices? Or between good and evil?" He waited for an answer, which was forthcoming as Penny pondered his question.

Penny smiled and replied, "Simply put, how can you have standards if there is no higher standard to judge them by? Nothing comes from nothing, and nothing could never be a standard for something. Something higher has to govern something lower. There has to be a light to shine on what is dark, or the darkness is indistinguishable." She stopped walking.

Dr. Hempstead stopped and smiled at her. "You are a maverick. If I am not mistaken, mavericks persevere in seeking out their answers, but divas feel entitled and go with what they already know. You consider yourself a maverick, which I think is a better endeavor, but it requires faith that the truth is out there." Then Dr. Hempstead dropped his arm as they left the park and walked back toward his office.

Penny wished for the feelings of comfort and safety from their first session, but she appreciated the fresh air and food for thought. "I agree. Faith, until everything turns around for me," she said. She almost wished he would just tell her that everything magically was going to be okay, but he did not say that—nor would he say that. She was starting to understand that there was a bigger design to her tribulations and suffering; something was unfolding in her life for which she could not account.

Dr. Hempstead smirked and shook his head at her bold manipulation of faith and God. "I am not sure 'everything' will turn around, as much as that *you* will be turned around. I would like to share with you something that gives me comfort. It's from the Bible, Matthew 11:28–30: 'Come to Me, all you who are weary and burdened, and I will give you rest. Take My yoke upon you and learn from Me; for I am gentle and humble in heart, and you will find rest for your souls. For My yoke is easy and My burden is light.' If it is faith you seek, then move closer to Him, Jesus, the Author and Perfecter of your faith." He went to open his office door, but Penny put her hand on his.

Pointing to her car and lifting her purse, Penny said, "I am leaving now. See you next week. Remember, our sessions are geared toward results with a specified duration and an endpoint. Do you have anything you want me to think about, like last time, before our next session?"

He nodded and slowly took out his phone to send her a text as Penny tried not to become irritated. When her purse vibrated, she retrieved her phone and read the text aloud: "'For we are God's masterpiece. He has created us anew in Christ Jesus, so we can do the good things he planned for us long ago.' Ephesians 2:10."

Dr. Hempstead added, "Sometimes we just need to trust Him, as our parent, our Father, for the things of the future. Also I'll add a question to that thought. Is happiness your ultimate goal, or will you have faith that God will provide for your needs and wants, including your desire to be happy when you trust in Him?"

Penny said, "That is a lot. I am also going to send you one of my dreams so you can analyze it. You can send me that last part in another text if you would like." She put her phone back in her purse and walked away.

As Dr. Hempstead unlocked his office, he kept his phone in hand so he would not forget to send her his final question.

Chapter 3

A Day in the Life

Once again Penny returned to the daily grind of her normal day, but things were different. Although she was still ignored by her coworkers for some insane reason, she felt different. She did not know how or why, but she had a little more joy in her heart. She wondered if anyone noticed or even if that mattered.

Again, it was too soon to assess her life. On one hand, she had her health, business, and some friends, but for the most part she was still alone—except for the good doctor. And on the other hand? She looked at one hand and then the other, as if she were a scale for justice, and quickly put the other hand behind her back. *Yep, too soon*, she thought.

Today it did not bother her, because she found just enough for which to be thankful. If God wanted her to spend her life alone, then she would be okay. She enjoyed her own company more than most people do. As for friendships and all the other things her life was lacking, she would have to trust God.

Penny occasionally reached out to her friends in Seattle, but not enough to satisfy her need for true friends. Ms. Magford understood, but most of her other friends saw her life as typical. People divorced, reinvented themselves, and moved on, making for themselves a better life—or at least working toward that goal.

Divorce is a horribly wicked thing, she thought, although none of her friends thought so. Most of her friends loved her but told her to move on with her life, but she told them she needed time to mourn and heal. They called her crazy and wanted her to move back to Seattle where they could take care of her. They were well meaning, but to Penny it seemed like a trap. She did not want to be wined and dined like in an old episode of *Sex in the City*. She just needed to question and understand her own existence and purpose as they related to life and even eternity. She doubted that she could ever find those answers in Seattle.

A couple of other things kept her from packing up and leaving. For one thing, she loved Northern California and her business was doing well. Nowhere else in the country, including New York and Los Angeles, would a house sell for an average of $2,200 per square foot. Although some condos went for more than that in New York, it did not financially equate, since as an average the South Bay real estate market was more fluid, even in a down market. Real estate rocked.

Penny was no longer comfortable in Seattle. Although she always missed her friends, she no longer considered Washington her home state. She loved the San Francisco 49ers, San Jose Sharks, and Golden State Warriors with a passion. She went to every game she could, despite considering it a sacrifice if she had to sit in the stands. Nevertheless she did not need a club seat to enjoy what came naturally to her. Penny thrived around other fans, kindred spirits.

She also loved the weather and people in Northern California. No one judged her or was critical of her circumstances. In fact, they did not think much about her one way or the other. She blended in with the locals and didn't want to go back to Seattle. For the most part, with a few exceptions, she liked the easy flow of California.

The few exceptions popped up at work. Some people were more pushy than others, especially clients in the real estate market, but she could not blame them for that. People were always bidding against each other for houses, even in a bad housing market. The really good properties did not even show up on the Multiple Listing Service until after they had a contract on them. Information usually traveled by word of mouth, and there were pocket listings that only the elite, well-seasoned real estate agent could obtain. Their clients were well established but frugal, which made it more interesting for Penny. The intricacies of this specific locale and the hustle and bustle of it added to the excitement of her professional vocation.

Unfortunately she was not the listing or selling agent for many properties, and she never received referrals from any of her clients. But Penny was good at math and figured she needed to buy or sell only one or two a month to substantiate her work as a real estate agent and give her a decent income. R&R, the firm for which she worked, required a minimum of two listing or selling contracts per month to stay employed.

Penny was on the bottom rung of her company's ladder, but she never missed her two contracts. Her favorite expression for her monthly accomplishment was to hold up the peace sign to her boss. Seeing her two fingers, he would always nod and smile, but this month it was different. When he saw her two fingers pointed up through his office window, he did not smile. Instead, he pointed two fingers down.

She immediately opened his office door and asked, "Hey, Rodge, do you have a minute." He nodded. "What's the matter? I'm not sure what that downward peace sign means."

As Penny watched, Rodger picked up something from his desk and rolled it around in his right hand. Then he looked her up and down and told her to have a seat.

Penny thought, *This can't be happening to me. Am I about to get fired?* She would argue for probation and a proven cause. She would not go down without a fight. She was a long-standing employee and had company rights.

Rodger, who usually kept to himself, seemed to be in a good mood. "I left you a voicemail that I wanted to see you anyway. Penny, if you don't mind me saying so, you look really professional today. It must be that suit."

Penny noticed that Rodger's eyes were extremely red. Agitated, she looked down at her attire and said, "Cut the crap, Rodger. Spending a little too much time behind that computer screen? What's on your mind?"

Despite Penny's abrasiveness, Rodger continued to act cool and looked at her in a way that gave her chills. "Well, I think we can talk about it over dinner if you would like," he said, looking at his watch. "We can invite one more person from corporate, Mr. Gilat, who works in Human Resources. We can meet for drinks around five-ish and then go for dinner at the Galloping Horse downtown—"

Annoyed, Penny interrupted him. "Son of a beach, Rodge. Do you expect me to go to dinner with you and your friend? This is harassment. I am not interested in drinks and your seven-course dinner. I know you and Mr. Gilat go for drinks all the time, but I am not interested." She looked for a reaction, but saw nothing.

Rodger pulled a bottle of eye drops from his desk and placed two drops in each eye.

Penny continued, "You just want him to be present so you don't get in trouble for going to dinner with me. Please tell me what you meant and what you want to say to me. Seriously, I have better things on which to waste my evening. I can do my nails and pick out tomorrow's outfit." Her cheeks were flushed and she was ready to walk out.

Rodge was taken aback. "One of your contracts fell out of escrow, so you did not have two sells this month." Once again he changed the peace symbol from two fingers to one finger and pointed down. "We have a regional position out of headquarters that would be well suited for the mild-mannered you. I was hoping you would agree to an impromptu interview."

With no words for her embarrassment, Penny managed to choke out, "Really? I am not being fired?" She had worked for this company for years and never doubted Rodge before, so why now? Granted, she never really had any lengthy conversations with him alone; mostly it was company meetings with staff. That's how it was in real estate—everyone pretty self-sufficient and on the move. Penny dropped her head, lifting it again only to mouth the word "Sorry."

With a sad little smile of disgust, Rodger continued, "It was corporate's idea. Apparently you still have a good reputation in the Seattle office. Mr. Gilat would have to sign off on it if he approves. You would be managing some of the regional offices. The position would involve some travel, and I am not sure of the other specifics. Thus the meeting with you, me, and Mr. Gilat." He paused to see if anything was registering.

Penny looked up, her cheeks still flushed, and said, "Thank you for thinking of me." She was not sure if she would take such an opportunity, but she definitely wanted to hear it out.

Rodger wanted her to know he was not behind this venture. Still disgusted, he looked again at his watch and said, "It wasn't me. Corporate thought you would be a good fit, so I am graciously extending the offer. You can think of dinner as a casual, impromptu interview—that is, if you are interested." He paused and tried to make eye contact, but Penny was fiddling with something on her skirt.

Penny looked up to see him staring at her. "Do you have scissors?" she asked. "Never mind. I will get it later. I am interested in hearing Mr. Gilat out. I would be especially interested in seeing a job description, although if it is still a work in progress, I'd understand why you have nothing to present to me yet. After all, aren't we all? Works in progress, I mean." Penny smiled through her embarrassment.

Looking shocked, Rodger pulled a piece of paper from

his desk and silently read from it. "Frankly, since your sells are not the best and R&R is raising the minimum effort requirement to three contracts per month effective next year, you might be doing yourself a favor. You may want to think about it, since this would give you a little more exposure to other R&R opportunities." He would have to sort through their conversation after Penny left.

She wanted to leave his office on good terms. Normally she would have demanded more information and better planning. Penny needed to have everything scheduled or things did not work for her. Even when clients found properties themselves and wanted to meet there for an open house, she would decline if the request did not fit concisely into her schedule. She would then schedule a proper showing of the property with the owner and the client at another time. Some clients had filled out surveys that said Penny was sometimes unresponsive. She knew it was because she did not always answer their phone calls or texts immediately.

She now felt obliged to honor Rodger's invitation. "Sure, no problem. I don't really have to pick out tomorrow's outfit tonight. I can wear this same outfit tomorrow."

Realizing that Penny was making another attempt at humor, Rodger said, "We will try not to spend too much time at dinner. You should have plenty of time for your nightly rituals." He was afraid it was going to be a long night.

Penny realized how snarky her comment must have sounded, but she was only trying to lighten the mood. "Especially since you liked it?" she asked. "My suit, I mean. You said I looked professional. Oh, you probably were thinking about the interview with Mr. Gilat, since I don't always dress for the office." Penny found herself becoming a little more cheerful with no self-awareness. She gave her boss two thumbs up.

Rodger wished he did not get to see this other side of Penny. He had never thought of her as socially awkward, but now that he did, there was no going back. He could try to chalk it up to her recent divorce. She had asked to take bereavement time, but he had told her that is not how bereavement works. He had thought she was kidding, but now he was not sure. "Are you going to be okay?" he asked.

Penny did not want to think about it. She pushed down the stray thread from her skirt as she got up. "Sure, this has been insightful. I will see you early tonight for drinks." She winked and pointed her index finger at him with her thumb stuck up in the air, like pointing a gun or shooting a rubber band.

Rodger had never before seen that expression on her face—or *anyone's* face. It was like an emoticon with all her teeth showing and her eyes wide open. She did not even blink. *Drinks may not be a good idea*, he thought. *It would be better to just have dinner.* Looking down at his desk, he said, "We should skip drinks and go straight to the restaurant, since this meeting has taken a little longer than I anticipated. I have some time restraints. We can get something with dinner."

Penny still had not loosened her jaw and at this point was starting to make Rodger a little nervous. He added, "I will text you the information for dinner—the location and time." He desperately hoped he could move up their dinner reservations.

Penny nodded and left the office. She had forgotten about her meeting with the good doctor that was also scheduled for that evening. She had known it was going to be a good day, and so far it had been.

★★★

Penny got into her car, started the engine, and plugged her phone into the charger. As one of her favorite tunes trickled through the speakers, she smiled and quickly turned up the music. Looking around the parking lot, she saw only a few other people leaving. She wanted to stick around and be dedicated, but she had to leave early for an appointment. Then it struck her. Her faced turned pale as she remembered that her appointment was with the good doctor. Well, maybe she could do both, the dinner with her boss and her appointment with Dr. Hempstead.

Penny arrived at Dr. Hempstead's office right on time. She looked at her watch and then at his office door. She could still make the appointment and be on time for her interview. Rodger had moved up the time, and she could fill her anxiety level rising. She hated having to rush to anything. She felt unprepared, but she could not give up her appointment with the doctor. He had grown on her, and she had become quite fond of him.

She would have knocked on the door, but it was already open a crack. She pushed the door open slightly to see the good doctor sitting at his desk with his head buried in a book—the Bible, if she was not mistaken. She would have expected him to be reading something a little more trendy, but as she watched him study, she realized that the book suited him.

Dr. Hempstead looked up and saw Penny standing in the doorway. "Come in, dear Penelope. I am glad you could make it. I was sure that you had not forgotten about me," he said.

Penny smiled and looked at her watch again. Dr. Hempstead walked toward the door, which Penny had already closed, and greeted her with a firm handshake. She then made her way to the couch and said, "I did almost forget. I have an interview after our session for a position within my company. I made a fool of myself with my boss, but he still wanted to get together for dinner. I had mistaken him for creepy even though I've known him for a while. I don't know why I behaved that way, jumping to conclusions and stupid assumptions. Sometimes I think everyone is creepy and they just keep it hidden until someone like me calls it out." Penny looked up sheepishly at Dr. Hempstead, whose head was turned slightly to hear her better.

Dr. Hempstead put his hand on his Bible and said, "It would do you some good to spend a little more time in God's Word. I'll tell you why. It helps you to think straight with proper constructs. It's good to know God's character, too. He keeps things straight when you ask for His help. Do you want to pray before you go to your interview? We could cut the evening short so you have more time to prepare."

Resisting the temptation to look at her watch again, Penny said, "Yes, let's pray. God is good and has good plans for me. I read that recently in Jeremiah 29:11. '"For

I know the plans I have for you," declares the Lord. "Plans to prosper you and not to harm you, plans to give you hope and a future."' I will take you up on reading more of the Bible. I have wanted to follow a reading plan, but time slips away." Realizing that was not the best excuse, she continued, "I could even listen at night through one of my cloud devices. There are Bible plans that help you listen to the Bible in its entirety within a year. I just have not set that up yet, but reading might be better than listening."

Penny talked for a little while and then prayed with Dr. Hempstead. Soon afterward she left the office, thinking that it was a great blessing to have someone with whom she could pray. She had such peace about her interview and dinner that she did not even look at her watch as she drove to her destination.

Chapter 4

The Interview

Penny pulled her Prius into a parking space right next to Rodger's blue BMW sedan 5 series. She was thinking of some snarky stereotype, but then remembered she needed to cut him some slack. Walking into the restaurant, she saw Rodger and his friend at the bar. She was eager to join them, but they grabbed their drinks and walked toward her.

Rodger told the hostess that they were ready for their table. Walking in front of Rodger and Mr. Gilat, Penny followed the hostess to the table. As she sat down, Rodger waited to push in her chair. She looked up at him and smiled as if to say, "Thank you," but he was glad that she did not make a fuss. Penny was not overdressed; she wore the same outfit from work, which was appropriate for an interview. *So far, so good*, Rodger thought, still holding his breath.

Looking at the two men now seated across from her, Penny was tempted to put her napkin in her lap. She was extremely hungry, but she did not want to seem overly anxious for dinner. *This could be fun*, she thought. But then her memory, which sometimes opposed any thought of fun, stepped into the picture and reminded her that she was not supposed to be happy. Penny was still looking for that change that would make everything coincide with her happiness.

The last time she had been at a restaurant in male company, it had been with Rick, her ex, and they had talked of their new lives. Now she could feel her eyes start to tear up. *I'm not ready for this*, she thought. *It's too soon!* But she quickly reminded herself this was a job interview, not a dinner date.

Noticing a single tear rolling down Penny's cheek, Rodger murmured "Hell no" under his breath. He was not going to ask what was wrong. In his experience, that question only led to an emotional response. He hoped her tears would clear up within the next thirty seconds. Otherwise he and Mr. Gilat could be in for a long night, which was the last thing Mr. Gilat needed before he flew back to Seattle.

Penny hoped no one had noticed the tear as she wiped it from her cheek. She had placed her phone in her lap. Her mission was to covertly check her messages, since she had not done so since leaving the office. Accomplishing that mission put her in a better mood. She then slid the phone into her purse on the floor and looked up to see the waiter standing there.

Clyde was not a friendly waiter. He was all business, although not professional, and he did not like to chat. "I would like to take your drink order," he said abruptly, looking right at Rodger, who lifted his hand and directed Clyde's eyes to Penny.

Penny had no idea what she wanted to drink, other than water with lemon. She paused and looked at the drink menu. She secretly wanted someone else to order first.

Clyde looked down at the small tablet that he carried in case he could not remember orders. He was supposed to memorize them, but he was still new at this and had not mastered the memorization part. "Oh, what would you like to drink?" he asked. "And if you want to order now, I can take entrée orders and add an appetizer to accompany your drinks." He sounded as if he was playing cards and had just upped the ante.

Amused by the waiter's matter-of-fact attitude, Mr. Gilat said, "I don't think we are quite yet ready for that, Sport. How about if I go first and order another gin and tonic?" He had just finished one from the bar and placed the empty glass to the right of his dinner plate.

Clyde grabbed the glass with his free hand. "Gin and tonic," he repeated to himself without writing it down.

Still looking over the drink menu, Penny realized she needed to make a quick decision. She told Clyde that she'd have the same and held up the menu, but then quickly took it back for a second look. "I'll have a water with lemon and ..." She paused, hoping something would pop into her mind.

Clyde circled the table to be closer to Penny. "A gin and tonic?" he suggested.

She knew that if she ordered a gin and tonic, it would be because she did not want to take the time to make a proper decision. She would get the drink but not have more than a sip. *No*, she thought, *I should order something I like*. But her mind was blank when it came to what she would like. She wanted to choose quickly, but nothing was coming to her. "Rodger, you choose," she said.

Rodger just raised his eyebrows.

"No, actually I think I'll have this," she said, continuing to peruse the drink menu without looking up. "Can I have a cranberry mojito—or better yet, mango?" Pleased with her decision, she happily surrendered her drink menu to the waiter.

Clyde thought about asking if she was sure, but it required too much effort on his part and he really did not care. He turned to Rodger and asked, "What would you like to drink?" He tried to smile, but it looked more like a smirk.

Clyde's manager had said that he, Clyde, needed to be more friendly with the customers. If he was more cordial, he would make better tips. Clyde could not understand why he would want to do that, since it would increase the time he was at the table—and, more importantly, the time the customers spent at the table. The less comfortable customers were, the sooner they would leave. It was about turning tables and making money. Even so, he attempted to grin as a token of cordiality.

Rodger pointed on the menu to a bottle of expensive red wine. He did not plan on drinking it all himself, so he ordered three glasses. He told Clyde to bring the bottle out with dinner, and that right now he would just have water with lemon.

Elated to see the price of the wine as he studied the menu, Clyde told Rodger it was a good choice and departed from their table.

The conversation began with polite exchanges about

the weather and events of the day. Soon Clyde brought glasses of water with lemon wedges and the cocktail drinks, and the conversation got a little more lively as the alcohol entered their bloodstreams.

Penny was well aware that she had not imbibed in a while, and she did not want to make a fool of herself. So when her mojito glass was empty, she told Clyde she would just wait for the wine, which he brought with the salads.

Rodger was glad to see that Penny had a social side that was not too loud. She did not drink too much, and she was not on the offensive like she had been in the office. Rodger thought that maybe he had been wrong about her. She was not uptight, but rather nonchalant about everything—including the interview, even as Mr. Gilat started to ask questions about her background.

When the conversation transitioned to interview questions, Penny excused herself to go to the bathroom. Although she didn't mind the questions, she realized that she had not given enough thought to changing jobs and moving to another state. She could tell that Mr. Gilat would be a great person for whom to work, but she also liked her current boss, Rodger. The new job would suit her many talents, and the job title was impressive since she would be a director. But change is hard, she thought as she met her reflection in the mirror.

Rodger took a sip of wine and a bite of salad. "So what are your thoughts so far? I hate to let her go, but the change may do her good. She has been through some rough patches recently, especially with her divorce. She is good with people, organization, and procedures," he said, aware that was a partial lie. "She would be a good fit even if she lacks experience." They had already talked about Penny as a candidate for procedural property director, but Rodger was more positive now.

Mr. Gilat laughed and asked, "So why is she so effing bad as a real estate agent? We hardly receive complaints about a realtor, especially after the clients find the house or property of their dreams, but her personnel file is an inch thick. She has not even been working for the company that long."

When Penny returned to the table, her face was red. She wasn't embarrassed, nor had she consumed too much alcohol. Sometimes her face just turned red for no apparent reason. "Thank you," she said as she sat down.

Mr. Gilat and Rodger looked at each other, a little puzzled, and Rodger asked, "Okay, why the thanks?"

Penny looked at him like he should know, but he obviously didn't—which made her wonder if she should not have thanked them. "Thanks for waiting for me while I returned from the ladies' room," she said, realizing immediately that there was no need for thanks.

There was that social awkwardness that Rodger had expected. He chuckled and thought, *Who thanks someone for waiting for them after excusing themselves to use the restroom?* "You're welcome," he replied. "Anytime."

The table was now quiet. No one felt the need to speak as they waited for their food. After a couple of minutes, however, Penny broke the silence. She had only one thing on her mind, so after taking two gulps of wine, she started talking, almost as if she was trying to talk herself out of the job. Everything that came out of her mouth was about her life and how she had made the decisions that had brought her to Northern California.

Mr. Gilat did not seem to mind. He had had his fill of alcohol and now gazed at Penny's blond hair, thinking about how silky and soft it looked. He wondered if he could ever tire of her blue eyes.

Rodger, on the other hand, was annoyed with both of them. The dinner was starting to run long as they waited for their entrees. Clyde had brought out an appetizer, compliments of the chef, while they waited. Then Clyde was bold enough to suggest another bottle of the expensive wine, and Mr. Gilat readily concurred.

The entrees came shortly after the second bottle of wine. Clyde served Penny first, as Rodger remarked on how everyone's food looked delicious. Penny placed her napkin on her lap, paused, and silently prayed before she picked up her fork.

Rodger, who had planned on expensing the dinner, changed his mind since the dinner had become more expensive with the additional bottle of wine. He now hoped that Mr. Gilat would pick up the check.

They were no longer in interview mode as far as Penny's qualifications were concerned, although Mr. Gilat would occasionally slide in questions and information. "How would you feel about moving back to Seattle again?" he asked Penny. He continued with a few details about the job, but he was now thinking that she was not qualified at all. "The team that would first report to you would be just a few direct managers from some of the local offices," he explained. "We would hope to grow your team from that starting point."

As their dishes were being cleared off the table, Penny became nervous. She looked at Rodger, but he just looked past her. She did not want to excuse herself to go to the bathroom again, since she had already been twice. Finally she could not stand it any longer. Even though she knew that she should take a day to think about the offer—and that she'd be angry with herself later for speaking prematurely—she blurted out her thoughts.

She leaned across the table, placing her fingertips on the table as if to tell them a secret. "I can't take the position. It sounds like it is just what I need and the company needs, but I can't do it. I am just now getting situated again. I have an exceptionally good therapist, and I like being a real estate agent." Then she looked down and mumbled, "Although I am on the bottom rung of the company ladder, and I am not very good at what I do." She lifted her head and looked at Rodger.

Stunned, Rodger hoped he could talk Mr. Gilat out of firing her later.

Mr. Gilat was not happy. He had decided that he wanted Penny around, and now he was not sure what his next move should be. "We have realtor positions in our Seattle office, and we could start you at base salary with bonuses if you were willing to wear another hat as well. You could still be an agent and accrue commissions, but you would also have a management position. Of course, the position we talked about earlier would have to be curtailed. You would report only to me, with no reports of your own." Pleased with his quick thinking, he knew he had just dodged a bullet.

Penny looked at her watch and shook her head, but thanked both Rodger and Mr. Gilat for a great dinner.

Rodger secretly wondered why Penny had picked real estate as a vocation. She was not a people person, and she had no finesse with her clients or her boss. Rodger, who had been at a loss for words, decided to lighten the mood. "If I only liked Seattle—oh, the opportunities. What do you think?" he asked, making fun of his colleague's attempt to hire Penny with the newly created opportunity.

No longer in a serious mood, Mr. Gilat said, "Yeah, well, no need. But I think I might move here to sunny Northern California." Once he said those words, the thought was anchored in his head. He was fast approaching forty and soon to be single. His fiancée had broken off their engagement so she could move to LA with her tennis partner, so maybe the change he needed.

Penny picked up her phone and launched the Uber app. There was an Uber Share about two minutes out and an Uber XL seven minutes out, so she decided to take the XL. When Clyde brought the check and handed it to Mr. Gilat, Penny went for her wallet, but Mr. Gilat waved his hand at her.

Penny stood up promptly and said, "Thank you. I just ordered an Uber. Does anyone want to ride with me?"

Rodger raised his hand and said, "I will. How about you, Mr. Gilat?" He felt okay to drive, but he knew the Uber was the smarter choice.

Penny was pleased. She looked at Mr. Gilat, sweetly waiting for his answer.

Mr. Gilat looked at her and then at the bar. He knew that he really should get back to the hotel, but he was tempted to stick around and make small talk with some of the locals, as was his custom when he was on the road. Looking at Rodger and Penny, however, he decided to go with them. It was the more professional thing to do, although it was not nearly as fun. "Thank you, I will take you up on that Uber," he said.

Having been tipped generously, Clyde was glad to see them leave. "Have a good night," he said in passing.

There it is again, Rodger thought. It was Clyde's peculiar grin, but this time culminating with most of his teeth showing. *Yikes!* It had been an awkward night indeed, and he would be glad when his head hit the pillow. I'll figure out what to do about Penny in the morning. Maybe I'll move up her performance review a week and put some monthly benchmarks, unrelated to sales, in place so that she'll have something in her file to show her competence. He was pretty sure Penny would have no regrets about the evening, since she was not the type to rewind conversations in her head.

After making sure that two additional people going to two other locations was okay with Diane, the driver, they piled into the Uber XO. Diane shared the concept of an Uber Share for information purposes only, and she was glad for the extra fares from fairly sober people. If one of them did mess up her car, the company would give her $500, which always came in handy. "Where to?" she asked.

Chapter 5

Dreams

That night, Penny tossed and turned, barely sleeping at all. With so many life events running through her head, she thought about who she was, where she was going, and whether she had given her future enough thought. She finally fell asleep at five o'clock in the morning.

Penny hated the feeling of too little sleep. She had dry mouth, and her head felt twice the size it should be for her body when she finally rose from her bed around seven thirty. Her legs felt like they had lead weights wrapped around them as she made her way to the bathroom. Staring into the mirror, she saw dark circles around her eyes. She had always thought people made up the cliché about bags under their eyes from lack of sleep, but the mirror reflected the unattractive truth.

The worst thing for Penny about a sleepless night was that it was purposeless. She felt robbed. Why couldn't God spare her from a sleepless night, when it was obvious that she needed to sleep? Her dreams were far from her, yet that was next on her list of things to do. She was to write down some of her dreams for Dr. Hempstead.

Penny remembered some of her dreams and knew she

had yet to write them down and give them to the dear doctor, although that was why she had originally gone to see him. She went to her desk, pulled out a piece of paper, and started to write what she remembered from her most recent dreams. She prayed that the Lord would bring back some of the details that she might have forgotten. She had made a dream journal for some dreams, to which she could refer if necessary. First she would record her most recent dream, from which she had just awakened.

Her dreams would be overwhelming if she told Dr. Hempstead about all of them at once, so she decided to write them down individually and discuss them with him one at a time. But how would she know if he was interpreting them correctly?

In ancient times, a king had a dream that he knew must be interpreted for the sake of his kingdom. When he wanted someone to tell of his dreams he would tell him to tell what is dream first or die. The decree they proclaimed made it impossible and improbable that anyone could tell of his dream. In the end, God provided a prophet that knew the dream and could interpret it. He told the king what would befall his kingdom in the years to follow.

She could ask the same of the good doctor but also thought it was impossible and improbable and she should cut the doctor some slack. She was not an "off with his head" type of person. No, she would just see the dreams through his eyes. She would see what he had to say. He was a trusted adviser—and even a friend, if she was okay with that. She decided Dr. Hempstead was a friend, but she would keep that to herself.

Penny's only dream the previous night had been silly.

She had dreamed about a cartoon character—Dastardly Dan, her archenemy—coming to life and dancing around as if making fun of her. She was now angry. *I feel as if I am at war with it, and I already know what I must do*, she thought. She wrote *Stupid* on the bottom of the piece of paper, underlined it, and then crumpled up her note. *That was a waste of time*, she told herself. *I don't need Dr. Hempstead to tell me what that dream meant.* The dream had been a warning to pay attention and take the threat of evil seriously, not to dance around it. But what evil spoke to her directly? She had no evil in her parochial life.

Penny thought about her divorce and how everyone gets divorced. How easy it was to part ways, to break an oath they had made together and settle things amicably. After all, marriage was as much a business agreement as anything else and was recognized as such in every state.

Somehow it was okay, though it had not felt that way at first. She and Rick, her ex-husband, were okay now, but was it really okay? She had been cajoled into thinking that moving forward meant not looking back at what had happened or how it had affected her thinking. She had even put behind her what God thought about it. What was done was done. No, she never thought about their divorce, and now she felt a bit threatened, as if she had taken it too lightly.

Was there any truth to the idea that working through her past would give her a better future? It seemed to Penny that she was supposed to cry, feel better, cry again, feel better again—over and over until her pain ran its course. *Rinse, lather, and repeat* popped into her head, and then her hair was clean minus the conditioning treatment that came later. But what if she needed to do more than that? What if she needed to reconcile some truth before she went on with her life?

Penny took the wadded-up piece of paper and laid it flat, working out the creases and then putting it into a folder that she labeled *Dreams*. She would get the doctor's take on that dream after all.

Penny did not want to talk about her marriage. After all, she was moving ahead and did not want to be stalemated at this juncture in her life. *But sometimes scars don't heal right if they still have junk in them*, she thought. She had never really stopped to ask herself if she was doing right or wrong by divorcing. She and Rick had only seen themselves as drifting apart. *Okay, doc, you can take this one*, she said to herself.

The phone rang. It was her landline. Not many people stilled owned a landline so close to Silicon Valley. It was that *ring-ring* with which she was so familiar, having grown up in a house with a phone in almost every room so as not to miss a call.

Her father's old-fashioned timepiece sat by the phone on the nightstand, where Penny liked to keep it. She sometimes would reach for it in the night, just to remind herself that everything would be all right. She was not sure whether it was okay to hold on to it, but she did anyway. She knew her father was not far away and that the Lord kept him. No, her father was not in the timepiece, but it was a reminder of how strong love can be—the ultimate love being the Father's love for her.

Her dad had taken to the Bible later in life and had often prayed privately as he read. She would open the door to his study and see him. He never apologized, and she would just close the door and walk away. Her heart now yearned for that fellowship with her father.

Penny had wanted the old couch that she and her father had sat on together for her living area, but her mother had had the good sense not to give it to her. With that couch, Penny would never leave her home. She would just stay home and drink coffee, then water and perhaps a cordial before bedtime, all the while sitting on that couch, destined perhaps to even sleep there until she eventually tired of it.

The phone had stopped ringing. Penny would have checked her messages, but the phone wasn't connected to a recording device. If it was important, they would call her cell phone. She then remembered that her cell phone was on both "do not disturb" and airplane mode. She liked to be doubly covered when she did not want to be disturbed and anticipated a good night's sleep.

When the phone started to ring once more, Penny picked it up. "Did you forget something?" asked Rodger. His voice sounded muffled but loud, although it was obvious he was trying to whisper.

Penny looked around the room for her purse and then her sunglasses. Yes, she had everything that she had taken to last night's dinner. Wondering what she had forgotten, she walked to her dresser while holding the phone, her ear pressed against the receiver and the cord stretching across the room. She looked down at her day planner, which was open to her daily agenda. *Oops*, she thought, *there it is, written in red marker so I wouldn't forget*. She was supposed to have met the Murphy couple at the warehouse. "Let me guess. You are at the office with the Murphys?" she asked Rodger.

The anger in his silence was clear, though Penny couldn't have told whether it lasted a minute or an hour. "I can explain," she said. "I did not sleep at all last night." She had messed up, but she had a hard time admitting it. "Tell them I will be there right away. I can be there in twenty."

Heavy traffic could be heard in the background as a muffled voice asked, "So how did you like it?" Penny could picture Rodger looking over his shoulder with his phone in hand. "I am covering for you," he told her. "Meet me back at the office in an hour. We have to work through some things."

Rodger knew that the Murphys were none the wiser. In fact, they told Rodger that they preferred him as an agent, since he was on time and had a thorough knowledge of the listing. He also was courteous, and they appreciated his unwavering attention. He talked only about the property and listened to their comments. They were glad that Penny had picked Rodger to help her out this morning. *Yep, none the wiser*, Rodger thought. *If only I was the client.*

There was dead silence on the other end of the line when Rodger ended the call. *Up a creek without a paddle*, Penny thought. There had to be something she could do to make up for this, but she could think of nothing. She did not want to be forced to take a job in which she had no interest, a job that she had already declined. At least she had not been terminated.

★★★

The road winding down the mountain was precarious

at best. Penny was not sure what had led to her decision to make the trek up, except for getting dressed too quickly, having nowhere else to go, and being too anxious to stay put. She had been out the door a few minutes after her call from Rodger. With extra time on her hands before she was supposed to be in the office, she had decided to drive and ended up on a road that led to the top of the mountain.

She had not gone too far up the mountain when she realized that she would be late for her appointment with Rodger, so she doubled back. *It will be okay to be somewhat late*, she thought, *since this is a casual but important meeting, but I don't want to be too late.* She wanted to be late enough that it did not look like she was worried about her job.

The mountain road was horrible. There was a trail of cars behind her Prius, and she would occasionally pull over at an overpass or lookout so they could pass. She also needed to be particularly careful of the inexperienced bikers in her lane. Bike enthusiasts were common on this Northern California road, but she noticed inexperienced bikers' fatigue as they wobbled up the mountain. *Good for them*, she thought, although they made her extremely nervous.

Lastly, although this was a romantic drive, Penny had no one with whom to share it. She noticed a group of bikers on the ride down and thought that at least they had each other. The leader looked back to make sure they were all still together. *It would be great if someone was watching over me*, she thought. She was glad to finally reach the end of the road.

At the end of the road, Penny was delighted to find

herself on the edge of downtown Saratoga, a romantic place with small wineries, restaurants, and boutiques up and down the street. She noticed her bank on the right-hand side of the road, so she pulled over to use the ATM and park. Her phone vibrated as if to say, "You are late!"

The text read, "I will be there before noon. The Murphys now want to see a couple more properties." Penny sighed. She was going to lose her job for sure. The Murphys were interested in a commercial property for one of their start-ups, which meant bigger bucks than if they just wanted to purchase a home. Rodger once more became the enemy as she blamed him for her future termination.

It wasn't quite ten o'clock, and Penny had to decide how to spend her morning. She definitely would make the most of her misfortune. After retrieving her dollars from the ATM and perusing the low balance of her checking account, she looked up and down the sunny street of Saratoga. Most of the stores were not open for business yet, but she had not eaten, so that would be her first choice.

She walked a couple of blocks and rounded the corner to find a cupcake shop. She had read that the shop had been in a televised battle to see who could bake the best cupcake. The shop looked and smelled delicious. They also sold a miniature cupcake, red velvet with white chocolate frosting, which had been a favorite of Penny and her ex-husband.

It had been a long time since such a small thing had reminded Penny of Rick. She had gotten rid of most everything to which they had been collectively attached:

old sweatshirts and ball caps, his old shirts that she had worn to bed, souvenirs from places to which they had traveled together, pictures, and a piece of jewelry for which she had never cared. She had even relocated and cut ties with their mutual friends, and although she hadn't made any new friends, she was better off.

She couldn't remember whether the saying went "Haste makes waste" or "Haste lays waste," but people in pain do things for which they cannot always be held accountable. Most of their things were in storage, in case she ever wanted to go through them—so whether it was made or laid, it was not a waste. Everything was there if she ever needed it, but that would be going backward.

Penny wondered how Rick was spending his time and if she ever crossed his mind. If she did, she'd never know it, because he never picked up the phone to call and say he was thinking of her, or even just to say hello. She was glad that he was okay and not missing her, but for the first time in a long time, she felt a forgotten twinge of pain. She kept walking.

The savory smells of bacon and fresh baked bread penetrated her nostrils. It was coming from the restaurant, the Bistro, that was now before her on her right. She did not care to read the menu posted outside. She was hungry and could make do with whatever they had, whether it was all vegan or all carbs. This time, her normal finicky desires would be pushed aside.

She pulled open one of the heavy wooden doors and went inside. Looking up, she noticed a tin ceiling that held the sounds of the hustle and bustle of the establishment. The waiters and waitresses scurried around carrying food and taking orders. *This looks like a fine place*, she thought. There was even outside seating, which she preferred. A hostess quickly approached her and asked "How many?" as if she were staring into a crowd.

Penny looked around and saw no one. She laughed a little and said, "Only me, and can I be seated outside?" The hostess smiled, grabbed a menu, and told Penny to follow her.

The phone vibrated once more in her faded Coach wallet. She would wait until she was seated before she returned the call. It was still vibrating as she reached her seat. She thanked the hostess and answered her phone, but she had just missed a call from Rodger.

A text appeared that said, "I can meet you earlier than expected. They did not want to see the other properties after all. Too expensive. It looks like you made your sell if they accept their offer. They want to make an offer on the warehouse near Roku in Los Gatos." His next text included a compliment: "That was a good find. Are you licensed to sell commercial real estate? We will talk when we meet. See you in a few."

Penny wondered, What should I do with Rodger? He's neither a villain nor a good guy. Like everyone else, he's somewhere in the middle. I do not always paint people in the best light, but obviously Rodger does not think well of me, especially after our talk in his office. Then again, they had offered to promote her. But what about now? Was he trying to steal her sale, although he did say it looked like she had made her sell? She had to wonder.

***

The parking lot was empty except for a few cars

scattered around. Penny decided to park her Prius in one of the reserved spaces at the front of the building, beside the spaces marked for those with disabilities. The building now seemed bleak and lifeless. *This has to be done*, she thought, opening her car door and stepping out. Head down, Penny walked into the office building as slowly as if she were walking into a funeral parlor. She hardly ever lacked confidence, because she was always about going forward and not looking back. But at that moment she definitely wasn't feeling confidence, that attribute that makes life a little easier whether it's supported by truth or lies.

Penny was wearing white sneaker mules that she slipped on and off at will. As she looked down, she noticed that they were a bit dirty. It was time to either bleach them or part ways. Suddenly realizing that she was looking down a lot, she lifted her head and saw Rodger fast approaching from down the hall. The small vegetable tray and bottle of wine he was balancing in his left hand were a surprise. He met her halfway down the hall and grabbed the door of the conference room with his right hand. They slipped into the room, Penny first.

Penny forgot her fear and lit up at the thought of celebrating her second sell of the month with Rodger. Although they would not close on the warehouse deal for another couple of weeks, even if it was all cash, as far as the tally sheet, they could count the sell for the current month if the offer was accepted by the seller. Rodger said it was a cheat, but it had been done on several occasions.

Their agency had yet to procure inspections, but the seller had his own set, so that should not be a problem in the negotiations. A seller's set could not always be trusted, but at least it gave them a baseline idea of how much work had to be done on the property. Fortunately the buyer's inspections would be made after the offer was accepted, so as long as the offer was good, she had made her monthly quota. Penny had a good feeling that the initial offer would be accepted, since it was ten grand over ask.

Also, the owner of the warehouse had a good relationship with Penny, and she practically had an exclusive listing on the property. He repeatedly had told her that if he did not already have a realtor, he would want her to be his realtor. But that could not be helped, because his wife wanted the commission and had become board certified just for that reason. His insistence was so sweet that it embarrassed Penny.

She and Rodger sat at the table across from each other. "I wrote the offer partially and sent the link, pdf format, to your Dropbox," he said. Then he went to the cabinet, pulled out two winglasses, and rinsed them in the sink. This was the only conference room with a wet bar and refrigerator, so it was usually restricted for use with clients, but today was the clear exception. Rodger set the glasses before them and poured from the inexpensive bottle of wine. He did not care to wait for her to sample it.

Penny lifted her eyes from the wrapped, mini-charcuterie board and looked at him closely. She again questioned his intent, since she could write her own offers, and wondered if he found her totally inadequate. "Do you think I can't write my own offers?" she asked. Realizing how wrong those words were as soon as they left her mouth, Penny laughed as if she had made a joke.

The combination of cheese, fruit, nuts, and meat on the wooden board made her hungry, although she had just eaten. Nervously she unwrapped a corner and took a couple of grapes.

Still standing, Rodger reached for the board and took it to the sink to rinse the fruit. Then he retrieved two plates from the cabinet and rinsed them too. Surprised to find that the plates had some food residue on them, he scrubbed them a little harder. When he looked back at her and said, "No, this is an amazing sell—aside from forgetting about the appointment," Penny blushed. Then it was his turn to chuckle.

"Oh yeah, in the midst of our celebration, I forgot," said Penny. She thought of the line from the poet Alexander Pope, "To err is human; to forgive, divine," but she knew that would cement her mistake. She was glad they had moved past it and on to their celebration. She finally saw Rodger not as just a quasi-okay boss, but as a great boss who had her back. *Another blessing*, she thought. *Maybe my luck is changing, or maybe it's still too early to tell.*

The words *odd duck* popped into Rodger's head. "They'd given me a lot of notes about structures they wanted to have included, which is automatically inferred in the initial offer. But I wanted to make sure, since sometimes things disappear—even structures—by the time the property is acquired. I just reworded it with legal repercussions," he said as he carried the plates and tray to the table.

Penny gulped half of her glass of wine and looked at her watch, thinking she had to be somewhere, but she did not. She had nowhere to go and no one to go home to, which for the first time in a long while struck her as sad. She missed Rick. She looked at Rodger and almost reached over to touch his hand, but realized that would be so misguided and unprofessional that she would never be able to explain herself. Still, she looked at him with teary eyes and a melancholy smile.

The wine bottle was half empty, though it was not the wine making her glad for the moment, but rather reminiscing about the past. It was good to work and have time pass quickly. It was good to have a boss who looked out for you. Rodger knew that look now, and he wanted to once again avoid whatever was coming next.

Rodger pulled a piece of paper from his pocket, unfolded it, and placed it before Penny. It was a flyer for a 5K, 10K, half marathon, and marathon. "It's my first half-marathon, and I've already signed up. I haven't started training for it, but I run about five miles a day, and somebody told me that if I'll work up to a ten-mile run, I should be good to go," he said. Until that moment, he had not intended to invite her, but she clearly needed something else to occupy her thoughts and energy.

The piece of paper had all the information that she would need, but Penny still looked confused. "So I guess it would be a date?" she asked. She took out her phone and took a picture of the flyer. Rodger smiled, but shook his head. Penny looked at him and thought, *His smile, his teeth are perfect. Why have I not noticed that until now?*

"No. Not only is that the last thing I was thinking," replied Rodger, "but that's also the last thing you need right now. The last time I checked, I'm still your boss, and that would make things awkward and unprofessional." Then he thought about the previous night and added, "That is, if you were to date anyone with whom you worked. I highly recommend you don't, for professional reasons."

Penny studied the piece of paper and said, "I don't run, but thanks for the offer. I don't even make it to the gym that often. In fact, I mostly walk, though sometimes I walk fast."

Rodger would have guessed that she had just come from the gym, and he was a little surprised that she did not make a habit of working out. He had assumed that not only had she been exercising, but also that she hadn't had time to shower before their meeting. "It would be just for fun, and there is a training guide online for beginners," he said.

Rodger's words—"No. Not only is that the last thing"—were slowly sinking into Penny's mind. *Was I just rejected?* she asked herself. *How does he know my needs?* She had not even asked him out. First divorced and now rejected, even with no intention of dating him, she asked herself, *Why me?* "Well, thank you for this celebration. I appreciate all that you did for me today, and I promise to return the favor if I ever have an opportunity. Oh, and I will also try to do better," she said, standing up.

His face went pasty white, an odd look for a man of East Indian descent, as he said, "No, that's not it. There's more." He realized that Penny must have felt rejected by him. "We have a runners' group. Actually, we have two. One is just a women's group and the other is mixed. The women's group meets at the trail right near your house.

They do cross training as well. They are just starting up and looking for someone else to run with them who is slow or hasn't run before now." All the facts flooded into his head, and he realized it would be perfect for her.

Penny sat back down, now that it did not seem as off putting. "Yeah, I'll do it if they need an extra person. I could run with others who are just starting out and may fall behind. It should be fun. Can you give them my cell phone number, and I will wait for their call before I register? I want to see how it goes the first couple of times before I sign up for a half marathon."

He did not want to say anything else discouraging, so he didn't. But he was pretty sure that she would end up doing a five- or ten-kilometer run for her first race. The rest of the wine stayed untouched, but they continued to talk. Rodger said, "It's my job to make sure you are okay. I need to know if you are struggling and what you need, and if I were to guess right now, you need fun." Rodger asked about Penny's home life and her family, and if she was in counseling.

"Yes, I have a great counselor. I met with him before I saw you last night for dinner," said Penny. "I am a mess, really, but slowly things are coming back into focus. I don't know if I should be volunteering this information since you're my boss, but you might have picked up on some of it by now. I am waiting for my luck to change."

There was silence for a minute, and then Rodger said, "We all go through difficult things at different times. None of us have it perfect, but I am not sure what luck has to do with it. I believe we make our own luck, and when things don't go our way, we can't let it define us. I also know that we have purpose outside of ourselves. We can't define our own purpose either, for that would be only a goal that we set for ourselves. But as we continue to seek it out, I believe we will find our way." He knew that was much more than what needed to be said. He should have stopped after "difficult times," but Penny was soaking up every word.

After a couple of hours, Penny realized the petite lunch was not only a celebration but also Rodger's way of checking in with her. She wondered if he had ever been offered a job in Seattle. To the best of her knowledge, he seemed over-the-top intelligent and super-professional, and he networked well with people. She would love to see him be a VP of their company or CEO of his own. She would definitely work for him.

Rodger was finally at peace. Penny was just processing her divorce and life in general, Rodger thought. She wasn't going off the deep end any time soon. It was his opinion that she had so much of herself tied up in her marriage that she just needed to learn to breathe again. He could work with her on her lack of commitment, as long as she was willing to work with him. He told her that their company, R&R, would be putting in place some benchmarks for their employees, so he would have some positive things to put in her personnel file.

"So you would be checking in more often than just at the end of the month?" asked Penny. Then she added, teasing him, "So we can meet here on Saturdays on a regular basis?" There it was again, his perfect smile.

"Yeah, no can do," replied Rodger. "Not interested in

giving up my weekends. That is why I took this position and partially gave up being an agent, though not the broker part. It's easier than stop and go. Maybe your next play should be thinking about getting your broker's license. You could have my job in a few years."

Penny shook her head. She had interest only in the moment for now—and keeping her head above water.

People kept popping into the conference room to say hi, but no one stayed. Sensing it was a private conversation, they teased Rodger and Penny about the wine. Only a few agents were still there by four o'clock, when Penny and Rodge finished their tête-à-tête. Then Penny went home to her empty apartment, and Rodger went home to two rescue pets. Tiger was a striped Pitt mix, and Albe was a white, part-Siamese cat. Other than his animal family, Rodger too lived by himself.

At Rodger's home, the sun was just beginning to set over San Francisco. He was excited that the day was finally over and his night was about to begin, but for the time being, he would just enjoy the view from his terrace. He had been looking forward to this evening for the last few weeks.

He had a date with Bellamy Amies, a woman whom he had met through one of his charity events. They had bid on the same painting, but she had gone beyond what he was willing to pay, even for a good cause. Afterward she had offered to sell the painting to him, since she had also bid on another item that she won. Rodger had agreed to take it off her hands, and she had agreed to dinner with him—but not in that order.

He would take her to his favorite restaurant in San

Francisco, and then they would hang out near Pier Street at one of her favorite places. He did not have anything else planned for the evening, but he was already hoping it would be enough that she would want to see him again.

Chapter 6

The Phone Call

Penny was thankful to be home with the rest of the day to herself. She was elated that she had met her work quota, because now she did not have to lose sleep over moving back to Seattle to keep her position in the company. And although she did not anticipate closing until next month, she looked forward to the commission and knew exactly what bills she would pay off first. Draping her sweater over a chair in the living room, she went straight to the refrigerator. She would celebrate her win with some sparkling grapefruit water and a plate of crackers and avocado.

Penny wondered if the buyers would have given her another chance if Rodger had not been there to take her place. She thought about the type of person he was, and she could not help but think very highly of him. He was good at networking, professional, and intelligent. Although she had not always thought of him that way, she realized now that not only was he a great boss, but he was also cut out for better things.

Seattle was a great city, and Penny wondered if Rodger had ever been offered a position at their headquarters like she had been last night. In fact, he would be a great

CEO of his own company, and she would definitely want to work there, maybe even as his joint owner. In real estate it was not uncommon for brokers to start their own companies if they could get around their signed disclosure agreements. She imagined their two names together on the same business card.

Then Penny's phone rang—and there it was, the life-changing phone call that stopped her dead in her tracks. Her little sister, Kalli, had been in a serious car accident, and Penny's mother wanted her home immediately. "Fine, Mom, I'll be there," she said, and hung up the phone.

Penny could no longer think about how much she dreaded going home, but only about her little sister and how much she missed Kalli. Penny had been wrong for carrying a grudge, and she wished she could take it all back. Her poor mother was estranged from all her kids, or at least Penny assumed that was the case. Honestly, she did not know. She spent the rest of the night researching the accident, hospital, and flights home. She did not want to leave in such a hurry, but she really could not assess the situation until she was there at the hospital.

The next morning, Penny placed her suitcases by the door. She had hardly slept, and her eyes were puffy as she unsuccessfully tried to keep from crying. If anything happened to her little sister, how could she not feel responsible in some way? Penny had not been there or even talked with Kalli. She had always found Kalli to be … well, difficult.

Rodger called Penny before six o'clock that morning, as soon as he listened to his messages. His date with Bellamy Amies had not gone as well as he had hoped, so he had gotten home early the previous evening. Nevertheless, he had agreed to go on another date with Bellamy, since she had asked him out this time. She had mesmerized him for most of the evening, until she began getting phone calls and things went south.

The first call had been to see if Bellamy wanted a friend to drop by the wharf unannounced to run interference. *Wow,* Rodger had thought. The other calls had been more business related. She had told him about the first call and explained that she had a lot of protective friends—and she air quoted "friends." He had not been sure what to make of "friends," but he had enjoyed her company up until the phone calls, so he had agreed to the next date, which would be later that week. Bellamy had to move some things around, but she had said that she wanted to do that for Rodger. He had not needed to check his calendar, because he would always make time for what was important.

Penny had left Rodger a voicemail telling him about her little sister, Kalli. "Please call me back at your earliest," she had said. Rodge had called her early that morning, but his call had gone straight to voicemail, so he had left a message asking what he could do to help.

Penny also left a message for the dear doctor, asking him to pray for her family. She said she was really sorry for leaving things with them the way she had, and that she had been thinking only about herself. Then she asked him to pray for that part of the situation as well, and asked if it would be okay to have their session later that week via phone.

Penny thought briefly about asking Rodger to fly

out with her, but that would appear too needy, and she did not want to deepen any feelings she might have had for him—not to mention the possibility that he might decline. Rodger was just a good, stand-up guy doing his due diligence as her boss. He had made it abundantly clear that he had no desire to date her. Penny wondered if she was even supposed to date anyone besides her ex-husband, if she wanted to do things God's way. But that was too much for her to think about right then anyway, so she was glad that nothing was weighing her down except her thoughts of her little sister.

There was a knock on the door, and Rodger was on her doorstep. He wasn't sure what he was doing there, other than to offer her a ride to the airport. Penny wrapped her arms around his neck, but then she let go when he said, "You will be okay."

"I'm sorry," she said, trying not to read too much into it. "My suitcases are right here, if you want to drive me to the airport. I'm glad that you're here."

Thinking that the suitcases could wait, Rodger stepped inside and shut the door behind him. "I can take you to the airport and, yes, whatever else you need. I also thought I could get a key to your place to water your plants or let your dog out." He looked around and saw that her place was vacant of life. "Or I could pick up your mail or just have it stopped for you. You know, you'll be okay." Then he asked, "When does your plane leave?"

Penny knew she was upset, so she said nothing. But there it was again—*okay. Who is ever "okay"?* she wondered. She could not get mad at Rodge since he did not know any better. She was not even angry with the doctor any longer. It was presumption, relative at best, and she would just have to deal with it. But she would not be angry, especially at Rodge.

Then Penny remembered a couple of things from her sessions, and instead of starting over with her thoughts and feelings, she decided to be "okay" for the time being. She hoped that Kalli would also be okay as she offered up a prayer for her little sister.

Penny's wristwatch had been a gift from her husband—silver plated with diamonds on the face. She wasn't sure if the diamonds were real, but it really did not matter since they were so small. The tennis bracelet that he had bought for her right before their divorce, on the other hand, had brilliant diamonds of at least half a carat and was worth a small fortune. She and her bracelet had parted ways about the same time as she and Rick had. She had flipped the bracelet off her wrist and let it sink to the bottom of a lake, as a statement of their failed love. She had no regrets.

The oven timer went off. "I should leave now," said Penny, walking over to the oven and turning off the timer. "I set the timer to remind me when it was time to go. My plane leaves in an hour."

Rodge thought it was weird that she would use the oven timer for that purpose, but even weirder that she left only an hour to get to the airport and through security. Panic set in for him, but he tried not to show it. He grabbed two suitcases and held the front door open for Penny, waiting for her to rush out the door, but she was in no hurry. He asked, "Where are we going, SFO or San Jose?"

Penny went back to the kitchen, grabbed two

bananas, and stuffed them into her oversized handbag. Then she took a small energy drink from the refrigerator and crammed that into the bag as well. The handbag resembled a carryon that a person would use for an overnight stay. Picking up her third bag by the door, she walked past Rodger and said, "My flight leaves out of San Jose. It should be okay. I have a half hour to get there and an hour to check bags, go through security, and wait at the gate." Penny tried to read Rodger's expression, but he was stoic. She made sure her apartment door was locked, removed her key, and gave it to Rodger.

He did not want to ask whether she had a spare key. He would just plan on picking her up at the airport upon her return. He pointed in the direction of his car.

"You can water the outdoor plants on the balcony and the one in my bedroom, which might already be dead," Penny said. "Also my mail and packages come daily, thank you."

As soon as they got to the airport, they got in line for curbside check-in. Rodger got out of the car and asked a family if he could cut in front of them to check Penny's luggage, since she was in a hurry. Penny thought it all worked out well. Penny made it through security and arrived at the gate to board just as they called for her group. Because she did not have an assigned seat, she was glad to make it onto the plane. She had wanted the bereavement fare, but she could not lie. She had a feeling that had to do with the closeness she felt to the Lord and her recent reverence for Him.

As soon as she was on the plane, a handsome gentleman asked if the seat was taken, which made Penny angry.

Everyone knew the answer to that question. If you did not have an assigned seat and the flight attendant did not seat you, you most likely did not have a seat. The gentleman was older, but still his question was unforgivable. "I'm not sure. Are you a sky marshal?" whispered Penny.

The man looked perturbed. He had never been tagged so quickly, and he smiled unwittingly at his own mistake. He took the seat beside Penny and lied. He did not see her as being perceptive, just good-looking and good company. His other choice was another unassigned seat in the back row where the seats did not recline. This was a last-minute assignment; otherwise he would have chosen his seat early or, depending on who was flying on the trip, had his seat picked for him.

The man had thought that Penny would keep to herself during their four-hour trip, but now that her curiosity was up, who knew? He was pretty good at sizing people up, but apparently not everyone. He thought he had lucked out with either a book scholar, sudoku expert, or magazine reader. He had eliminated movie watcher, music listener, or person flying for business who would be on their computer the entire flight, only to break for lunch and a TV show. The telltale sign was that no computer was poking out of her bag, nor did it have a separate compartment to hold electronic devices. There was a folded magazine sticking out of her purse, which looked to him like an overnight bag.

Penny was excited to have a sky marshal sitting next to her, and she was glad for the distraction. "Well, if you were a marshal"—she paused for moment to get his attention, although he did not look directly at her—"you would be in good company." She pulled out her magazine and pointed to her name, Penny Marshall, on the front cover.

The man looked around at the other passengers and turned to the back of the plane, but it was too late to switch and there did not seem to be any other seats vacant. "So, Penny Marshall," he asked, "Do you fly this airline often? My name is Howard, and I pilot private planes for a living."

I was right! I was right! was all Penny could think. He had to say something aeronautical to explain why he was able to seat himself and had some familiarity with the airlines, but he was a marshal. *This could be a fun trip!* She was not sure if she should thank God, but she did—another mystery to occupy her mind and time. "So do you have your own plane, and what type of plane do you fly when it is not grounded?" asked Penny. This was better than the sudoku puzzle at the back page of her magazine, on which she would have a hard time concentrating.

Howard knew where this was leading, but he thought, *What the heck? Maybe I can steer the conversation in a more interesting direction.* "It's a 400XPR," he said. "I pilot for just one specific group and individual. The plane stays in the bay unless I am authorized to take it somewhere." He hoped that would be the end of the questions.

Penny had to be convinced she was wrong before she would let it go. She smiled and looked at her magazine teasingly. "So your plane is a Beechjet Hawker? I heard those are nice. It's a small jet, though, to be flying for someone. Usually the owner will fly it themselves." She looked at him like a dog with a bone.

The banter continued for at least an hour until Penny finally tired of her own questions. Unable to steer the conversation in any other direction, Howard had made no fewer than three trips to the bathroom. He wanted off the plane, not only because of his stomach problems, but due to the incessant questioning which could have been the cause of his sudden illness. Although he tired of their conversation he would still ensure that he had Penny's number before he left the plane. He already knew the address where she lived from the magazine cover, and it was not far from his own home.

The plane circled and finally let down its landing gear. Howard could have said something about the plane's mechanics and operation, but he did not want to perpetuate the lie. He would come clean and hope it would not cost him his job. He'd do it just as they were getting off the plane but before they said how nice it had been to meet each other. He leaned into her and told her that she was right.

Penny's mind had already gone back to Kalli and being home. She had forgotten about the sky marshal. He turned to face her and said, "You are perceptive. Can I get your number? It would be for personal reasons."

She was shocked and wanted to say yes, but she had doubts. She reluctantly gave him her mother's phone number, as she would be staying with her mother. She would not want to have her number changed at a later date, but just told him that it was a number where she could be reached in case of an emergency.

He thanked her and said it had been a pleasure sitting next to her, which was a lie.

★★★

They exited the plane together, but then went their separate ways. She texted her mom that she had landed. The next text read, "I'll meet you outside of baggage. I am wearing a red coat." Penny was putting on her coat and looking for the nearest bathroom. She hoped her mother hadn't forgotten, but with so much going on, it would be understandable if she had. Penny would just find another mode of transportation.

Penny's phone rang. She had stuck it back in her pocket as she walked. It was her mother, and Penny's first thought was that she had forgotten. "Hi, Mom. It's not a problem. I can take an Uber to the hospital." Her heart went out to her family, and she was sad that she had not been there for them sooner. "Or is Coby coming to pick me up? I was thinking I would meet whoever outside of baggage or, if they wanted to come inside, at the baggage claim. I should be at B4, if you want to text that to Coby." *Oh shoot*, she thought, *I'm going to see that guy again.* But then she remembered that he had put his luggage in the overhead compartment, probably in accordance with his job.

The train approached quickly, and as soon as the doors opened, people exited from the other side as other people piled on from Penny's side. "I am sorry to do this to you," said her mother, "but your husband—excuse me, your ex-husband—was here to see Kalli. When he asked if there was anything he could do, I said that he could pick you up at the airport."

The train jerked as it started to move. Penny was in the middle, holding on to one of the poles, and she nearly dropped her phone. She turned her back to the people closest to her and said in a loud whisper, "Mom, I can't. How is that a better idea than me taking an Uber? I can't see Rick right now. He's the last person I want to see. He will make me angry on top of being sad. Is it too late to tell him not to come?"

The train came to a halt, but she was not sure it was the right stop. Then the announcement over the loudspeaker said it was the stop for baggage and ground transportation. Penny got off and followed the crowd. She saw the sign overhead for ground transportation and baggage, so she continued straight down the corridor with many other travelers. She listened as her mother made excuses. "I don't know what an Uber is," her mother said, "but I know Rick is a safer bet. Besides, he insisted, once I told him you were flying here and it helps me out."

The phone was the only thing Penny could throw. Instead she squeezed it as hard as she could and gritted her teeth at her mother. "Ugh, Mom, I just need you to call him and let him know that I found another way to the hospital." She was nearing the main part of the airport. The escalators took her down to baggage, but she could walk straight out to transportation.

"Penelope, act like an adult. Kalli is touch and go, and I need you to think of somebody besides yourself right now. Besides, he is coming back to the hospital," said her mother. She knew she was not Penny's favorite person, but she still was her mother. "Sorry, but he will be there in about twenty minutes and meet you outside of baggage. He just texted me. Is there anything that you'd like me to text to him for you?"

Penny's object of aggression was now herself, rather

than the phone. How could she have been so dumb as to not make her own arrangements? Of course her mom would want to stay at the hospital with her sister. "Mom, I am so sorry. You are right. I am acting like a child, and I should be glad for Rick to pick me up. I just wish it wasn't him." Penny did not know if that last part detracted from her apology, but she was thinking out loud and processing the prospect of seeing her estranged husband. With a few minutes to make herself presentable, she stepped into the bathroom.

"Penny, it sounds like therapy is doing you a world of good," said her mother. "I will be glad when you get here."

Penny ignored the comment about therapy, since it begged the question "Why did you say that?" or "What did you mean by that?" She simply told her mother that she could not wait to see her as well. Then she ended the call and texted her ex, "Greetings. Let me know when you are outside baggage. I am wearing a red coat. XXXOOO." He may or may not have found that funny, but she was betting on the latter, and chuckled.

The bathroom mirror had streaks that ran horizontally. She worked with what reflection she had as she washed her face and reapplied her makeup. She couldn't do much about her hair. Whether she clipped it into a little blond ball or put it in a ponytail, it still was going to look oily, since she had not showered. She had a few minutes to spare before she was to meet Rick, so she texted Rodge that she had made it okay, attached a selfie, and thanked him.

Rick was waiting patiently as Penny approached the car. She looked down at her silver watch to see whether he was early or she was late. Panicking as she looked at her gifted watch, she turned around so she could unlatch and slide it into her pocket without him noticing. Then she pretended to look for his car in the other direction.

Rick got out of his car and said, "Penny, I am over here." His red Mercedes had been a gift to himself that Penny had applauded, not anticipating that it was the first of a series of changes that would culminate in something she would not understand. She waved and walked over to his car as he held the driver-side door open.

Penny slid in and thanked him as he shut the door. "Rick, it's really good to see you. You look"—she paused, looking at him in the dim light—"okay. I can't really tell since there is not much light, but I'm sure you're keeping up appearances." *Oh, that did not come out right,* she thought.

Surprised, he laughed and asked, "How are you, Penny? It's been awhile, and with or without light, you look great." He knew that did not come out right, but he also knew it was true.

Penny blushed. Her hands were on her lap, but she really wanted to be texting—anyone, anywhere. She was so anxious that she hoped she wouldn't throw up. That was not one of her things, but she really felt nauseated. "I'm doing okay for the first time in a while. I'm not sure if my karma is changing, but I don't think that's important anymore. I'm not defined by my situation." Suddenly aware that she definitely was going to throw up, she asked, "Can you pull—?" Without time to complete her request, she opened the door and threw up on the side of his car and the pavement.

Fortunately the car was still moving at a crawl as Rick inched into the fast lane. His eyes widened, he asked, "What can I do? I can wait before we hit the freeway." He pulled back over into the slow lane, reached behind her seat for a bottle of water, and handed it to her. When Penny opened the door again and finished throwing up, Rick reached over and pulled napkins from the glove compartment.

The driver of the car in the adjacent lane made a face and said something, probably assuming that Penny was drunk since it was already late afternoon. The old Rick would have given him the bird, but that Rick was long gone. He and Penny had aged together. At twenty years old, he had been ambitious and sometimes angry, whereas she had been less ambitious but more worldly. They had complemented and counterbalanced each other.

Penny wiped her mouth with a napkin and said she thought she was finished, but then she threw up one last time as they approached the toll booth. "This time I am done for a while," she said, and she downed the bottle of water. She then had to pee, but that could wait until the hospital. She wished she had showered, as she started to smell less like vomit and more like body odor. If only she had known she was going to see Rick. She had not anticipated talking to him, much less seeing him while she was in town. She could only wonder what he must have been thinking of her.

The hospital parking lot was full, so Rick parked in the garage lot across the street and they walked over. He was good, making sure she was okay and filling her in on the details about her little sister, though he did not stand too close to Penny, especially in the elevator. He remembered the layout of the hospital and where her sister's room was. Penny longed for a bed and a shower, but she most desperately wanted to see Kalli.

The room was in the intensive care unit, just through the double doors to the left. Rick hung back and let Penny go first. When she hugged her mom and asked how Kalli was doing, her mother said that Kalli was not waking up. With tears running down her face, Penny went to Kalli's bedside and held her hand. "I'm here now and I'm so sorry," she said. "I'm so sorry. I never meant to leave you."

As Rick listened, his eyes welled up with tears. He entered the room and sat by his ex-mother-in-law, put his arm around her shoulders, and pulled her close. She was crying too.

Chapter 7

Nowhere to Go

Penny was back at Kalli's side early every morning waiting for her sister to wake up, and finally she did. With a twitch and then a toss, Kalli's eyes fluttered, and in the fullness of time she returned to consciousness. "Mom, she's coming to," said Penny. Her mother was napping.

Kalli's eyes opened and she said, "Hi, Penny, I've missed you."

Unable to speak, Penny told herself not to break down and cry. She just held her sister's hand and smiled.

Kalli continued, "Are you here because of my accident? I had the weirdest dream. It was so true to life. I was happy, like a different type of joy. I was in this beautiful white dress, but I was in a wheelchair. I was getting married to Sid, a guy with whom I work, but we are just friends. Have you ever had a dream like that, so real?"

Tears were running down Penny's cheeks, and she was trying hard to keep it together. The empty room filled up quickly, as first nurses and then a couple of doctors rushed in. Mom was wide awake by then, and Kalli was in shock at all the attention. Penny knelt by her mother's chair and managed to say, over and over again, "Thank God."

One of the doctors was conducting a battery of physical tests and asking Kalli a lot of questions. But as she got over the shock of such an inordinate amount of attention, she became annoyed with the questions. No, she was not sure what day it was. Unable to make eye contact with Penny, Kalli started to realize she was missing from her view—and then there was the pain. "Make it stop, make it stop," she cried.

When the doctor ordered twenty cc's of morphine, Mom spoke up from behind one of the nurses and protested, "That's too much. Start with half of that. She might go back into a coma." The doctor agreed, and with a smaller dosage of morphine in her bloodstream, Kalli calmed within minutes.

Kalli laid her head back on her pillow and went to sleep. The room eventually emptied, but the doctors promised they would be back to get her for a CT scan and other diagnostic tests. Kalli was going to be hospitalized for a long time, while the doctors worried about internal bleeding and vital organs. Mom overheard one of the nurses say the word *miracle*, but she couldn't care less—she just wanted her Kalli back.

Penny and her mother stayed with Kalli as she was moved to the critical care unit. Rick came every day to check in with them, and he kept telling them that Kalli's survival was a miracle. No one wanted to hear that, although they continued to pray and thank God.

Since she had nowhere else to go, Penny moved out of her hotel room and back into her old room at home with her mother. She missed her father more than anything.

Penny went to his study, which was unchanged, and sat on his old couch and wept. How could he have left them, even if it had been his time? Her whole life would have stayed the same, and she would never have left her family or her marriage. *Everything would been okay*, Penny thought. But a quiet voice corrected her, and she knew that it was true. God's timing is not only right, but also perfect.

Penny soon realized that Mom was not the person she remembered. Both she and her mother had grown into different people. Calmer and more self-assured, her mother had grown stronger and her faith was deeper. Penny believed that God had grown her mother's faith through her father's passing and her own faith during their separation. As Penny examined herself, she realized that she was not as self-obsessed.

Usually around midnight, when they were both back from the hospital and could barely stay awake, Penny and her mother found time for fellowship. They prayed, drank decaffeinated tea, and talked about their lives. During her divorce, Penny had really missed the friendship that she now had with her mother. What she appreciated most was that her mother accepted her as the woman she was now, flawed but always her child.

They talked about the Lord mostly, and the different things God was doing in their lives. Penny's mother talked about her study of Romans, and how the Lord was moving her from grace to more grace. How her obedience, especially with Kalli, meant trusting in God, the importance of fellowship, and how thankful she was for her fellowship with Penny. Fellowship, her mother explained, had been part of her Romans study and was essential to the believer's life. Believers are part of the body of Christ, and everyone plays a part equally. There are no small parts. She went over scripture and some of her studies with Penny, who in turn went over them with the good doctor, who had become her closest confidantes via their video chats sessions.

***

The new hospital room was different from the rooms Kalli had stayed in while she was being monitored all the time in ICU and CCU. Penny still visited with her daily, but no longer for the whole day. She was now telecommuting and trying to catch up on the work which Rodge had obtained from corporate. It helped make ends meet while she was in Seattle.

Rodge had flown a couple of times on business and stayed with Penny and her mom. He even had the pleasure of meeting Rick, Penny ex-husband, whom Penny tried to avoid. Penny pressed Rodger on his opinion of Rick, but Rodge said he had no opinion. But since he never said that he liked Rick, Penny was inclined to think that he was not fond of him.

When Penny arrived at her sister's room for her final visit, Kalli was engaged in a conversation with Missy, the young woman with whom she now shared a room. Missy was about Kalli's age and had also been in an accident, though not a hit-and-run like Kalli's. In both accidents, the other driver had been at fault. In Kalli's accident there had actually been two drivers. The first driver had gotten away, but the second driver, who was cited for reckless driving, was hospitalized. Missy had been a passenger in a Prius driven by Darren, her boyfriend, when the driver of a short-semi truck had run a red light and blindsided them.

Kalli and Missy had both survived, and Penny kept saying Missy's story was a miracle, but Kalli hardly thought so. Both Kalli and Missy were blessed to be alive. Darren had more extensive injuries, but he too was healing. Penny said it was a small miracle, but Kalli said Penny should stop talking to their mom.

Aside from her occasional rants Kalli thought of Missy as a less annoying roommate than most. Missy promised to keep in touch when they parted ways. Kalli wished she wouldn't, but she was not sure how many of her own friends she would have left when she got out of the hospital and just perhaps she should be happy for the one, new friend.

The life of a handicapped person would be different indeed. Penny asked if her sister wanted her to move back home, but Kalli said no, not necessary. They could talk on the phone, and that would suffice. Penny laughed at her stoic response.

Many of Kalli's friends visited from time to time. They would stay and chat, but she wondered if they came for the sake of their own consciences and protocol rather than because they were truly devoted to their friendships. If the situation was reversed, she could not be sure what her motives would be, but she would definitely stop by to see that person.

Penny knew that Kalli's fears were many, and she occasionally recommended that her sister talk with her dear doctor. Penny wrote down her doctor's number, and told Kalli how they had travailed on many of her phobias and issues, like estranged relationships.

She also added that in her experience, Kalli did not need to worry about friends. "True friends," Penny said, "like family, walk in when everyone else is walking out. It's always hard to find friends who stick with you through thick or thin. Speaking of which, you keep getting buzzed by Sid. I have not met him yet. Why don't you let him come and see you?" She handed Kalli her phone.

Kalli showed no interest in the phone. "No, I don't want Sid to come visit. We are not friends. We just worked together.", said Kalli. Penny knew that was a lie.

The chair next to Kalli's bed was often moved away by the nurses, but it was still there when Penny arrived, which meant that someone had recently been there. Penny sat down, pulled the chair close to Kalli, and asked, "Do you want to talk about your dreams? I have dreams all the time. I realize some of them may have significance, while others do not. My friend Ms. Maggie, who has gone to be with the Lord, recommended my dear doctor. I decided that I did not need to decipher my dreams as much as I needed to trust God, but you should talk with him if you don't want to trust me. He'll tell you if there is any truth to your dreams."

Kalli was already looking at her phone, texting one of her friends. "No, you're odd that way. If I have any dreams, I'll call your dear, good doctor. I am glad he was able to help you after you got dumped by Rick. By the way, Rick is a really nice guy. See those flowers over there? Those are from him. Every time the flowers begin to wilt, he brings me fresh ones. He comes by when you're not here, and he'll bring a deck of cards and play games with me. He's really fun." She paused and then added, "I guess you can't win them all."

Penny suddenly realized why she and her sister weren't closer. She moved her chair farther from the bed, stood up, and asked, "What do you mean by 'You can't win them all.'? Oh never mind, I came to tell you that I will be leaving soon. Are you sure Rick didn't just want the scoop on me?" She glanced at Kalli's bedside table and saw a worn deck of cards.

Kalli dropped her phone into her lap and glared at her sister. "Okay, Penny, you were always a little conceited. You're not the topic of our conversations. He shared with me his feelings, but I told him nothing since I don't keep tabs on you." Kalli hesitated before continuing, "I was hoping that since my life is changing, maybe you and I could stay close again, like when we were younger. I like you better now than I did when you lived here, and I also like Rick much better. He's really cute."

The deck of cards is laden with gold glitter, thought Penny. *Just like Rick, a lot of glitz.* She grabbed the deck, moved her chair close to Kalli's bedside again, sat down, and dealt eight cards for each of them. "Crazy eights," she said, "but maybe I'm supposed to deal eleven cards? Kalli, I will be here for you no matter what you need, but watch out for Rick. He usually wants something. He keeps asking me out for coffee or just to meet up. He wants to talk, but I still need to figure things out. It's complicated." Seeing Kalli's head perk up, Penny added, "Don't relay this information. Just stay out of it, little sis. I love you."

Kalli smiled that of a chestier cat and asked for spades as she laid down the eight of diamonds. Penny drew another card. She stayed another forty-five minutes before catching an Uber for the airport.

On Penny's flight back, Howard sat beside, but this time on purpose. "Hi," she said, and he greeted her back. "Are you on or off the clock?" she asked. Howard told her he was off the clock.

Their conversation had become much more casual since they periodically talked on the phone together. He had called Penny ahead of time and asked if he could make arrangements to fly back with her. Penny readily agreed since she enjoyed talking with him. The stewardess walked by to make sure everyone had properly fastened their seat belts. Penny looked at her lap and nodded.

"What do you think?" asked Howard. "When we get back, you and I could go on a weekend cruise out of San Francisco as friends?"

Penny shook her head no, and immediately felt unwell. They had agreed to be friends, but nothing more. Back home, Rodge and Dr. Hempstead, were the only other two people she considered to be her friends. She wished for more girlfriends, like she had in Seattle, but if she had to make due, Howard was good company and very amiable.

Howard had been looking forward to this flight for awhile. He had flown four hours there, so that he'd have their flight back together. He actually hated flying except for his job, thus the mention of the cruise. But now he had to think of something else that they could do together that would be less intimidating for Penny.

The stewardess asked the man in the aisle seat to fasten his seat belt. When he thanked her and Penny heard his voice, she immediately turned around and exclaimed, "Rick, what are you doing on this flight—and so close?" That last part just slipped out. Her stomach tightened.

As the stewardess continued down the aisle, Howard asked, "He's your ex?" When Penny nodded, he turned around—not pleased. Rick held out his hand, which Howard accepted.

A young woman in her twenties, seated in the row in front of them, took off her headset, looked behind her at Rick, and laughed. Penny wished she would mind her own business. The person in the seat directly in front of Rick had his eyes closed as his head rested on his neck pillow. He opened one eye, turned his head slightly to the left, and then closed his eyes again.

Penny grabbed a bottle of water and some cheese and peanut butter crackers from her purse. She started to eat and sip her water as Howard carried the conversation. She was pretty sure it would keep her from throwing up, but if not, it was fewer calories ... not that she was counting.

The plane started to taxi. Penny would be trapped on this plane for too long. She took out her magazine. Howard looked at her magazine, then at her, and raised his eyebrow. She motioned for him to keep talking to Rick, which made no sense to Howard, so he did the only sensible thing and asked Rick, "So do you want to switch seats?" Rick nodded, and they quickly traded seats. Penny objected, but it was too late. She was sitting next to Rick.

Rick looked over at the magazine on Penny's lap and asked, "So you still like that rag?" Usually he knew to avoid Penny's pissed-off expression, but not today. "Hey, I'm sorry about this, but you've been avoiding me," he said. "Your mom is a sweetheart. You and I should have spent more time with the family when we were together. She gave me your itinerary, and I tried to get the seat next to you. It was taken, so I switched with the man in 12A after you were seated."

Penny ate another cracker and took another swig of water. She knew him too well. "Yes, Rick, I still read the *American Conservative;* it's better than what you don't read, which is everything! I also know the man whom you ejected from his seat, and yes, I was looking forward to the flight until you showed up.", she said and took a deep breath. "Can you just go away? No one likes you, especially me." Although Penny was trying to talk softly, the young woman in the next row obviously heard her. The woman mumbled, "Ouch!" and chuckled as Penny started to feel a little light-headed.

Rick looked back at Howard. Howard pointed at Rick's seat, his own seat, and then back at Rick's seat and waited for Rick's reply. But Rick, who did not want to switch back yet, shook his head.

Howard did not like complicated things. After all, he was a sky marshal. His job was to alleviate complicated situations or at least watch out for them. His job involved a different type of complication, and he knew it when he saw it, but in general he was a simple man with simple tastes. He was not sure where Penny fit in, but he desperately wanted to find out.

Cheese and peanut butter crackers were a new thing for Penny, who had discovered them at the office in the vending machine. She offered one to Rick, since she had another pack in her purse. Where was Rodger when she needed him? The good doctor would be a wonderful flight companion. Howard could be suitable for conversation, but she knew there would be tension and perhaps pressure. Why now did Rick appear? She lifted up her question to God.

Rodge came to mind again. He was turning out to be a much better friend than Rick had ever been during their marriage. Rick had ambition, was good-looking, and loved adventure, but he lacked the sentiment, maturity, and commitment that most relationships required. They had mutually agreed to separate and divorce, so she must have lacked some of those things too.

Rodger's cool exterior and pragmatic ways would be a comfort about now. Now that they were in the air and she couldn't text him, she put her phone in airplane mode. She looked around the plane for him just in case, but remembered his text that morning telling her to have a safe flight and to call him when she landed so he could pick her up. She had forgotten about Howard, who might have wanted to give her a ride home—more pressure.

The cheese and peanut butter cracker did not look appetizing to Rick, but he took it and thanked her anyway. He raised it as if he was toasting, but she stuffed hers into her mouth and took another sip of her water. Although it was still in knots, her stomach no longer felt tense.

Rick said, "How is it that you could not find time to talk with me the entire three months you were in town? This trip could have been avoided, and Howard and I would have never had to meet. Now I have met two men in your life, Rodger and Howard. The only person left is the 'good doctor'—and I hear from your mom he's been a godsend."

Penny's phone buzzed. *Impossible*, she thought. She looked down and saw three texts on her screen: "Safe travels 4u and family. See u soon," with praying hands from the doctor. "Love u sis. HAVE FUN," with hugging hands from her sister. And lastly, "Safe travels. I will be praying for you," from her mother. She looked at her phone, which was now off airplane mode. The indicator went back to no signal, and again she switched back to airplane mode. She was thankful. Somehow the messages came through and she was at peace.

Penny's countenance changed, but Rick's words still seemed like a bunch of rhetoric that she could do without. However, she was on the plane now with him, so she would hear him out. That would be one less thing she would have to worry about in the future. She said to Rick, "The good doctor is a blessing. He has helped me through a very difficult time in my life. How about you? Are you seeing anyone?" The question made her sad and angry at the same time.

The window seat next to Penny was empty, which was unusual for a flight of that size. Rick stared out the window and answered slowly, "Yes, I was. But she, my counselor, led me down a rabbit hole. She kept telling me that it was time that I moved on from my past and started new. She signed me up for all these singles' activities in the area, which were just classy hook-up places. It made me feel dirty, everything felt contrived. After the first excursion, a boat trip, I felt trapped. I left by myself as soon as we got back to shore. Don't get me wrong—I love hiking, rafting, and weekend tours. But these singles' events were a waste of my time and depressing."

Penny put her hand on his and said, "I know it's awful. I'm still working through everything, but it seems like things are different from when we first started dating. I'm not focused on being single, but I have been focusing on God's purpose for me. There are things we strive for, but it seems meaningless to me. Have you ever wanted more from life?"

Rick seemed intrigued and leaned closer to her. They continued to talk. Howard could only hear whispers.

The woman who was catty-corner to Howard now lost interest in their conversation and placed her earphones back on her head. Howard, too, was trying not to hear their conversation. He put his noise-canceling headset on, placed a pillow with an attached hoodie around his neck, and closed his eyes. He looked stupid, but at least he couldn't hear anything.

The sun through the window was blinding, so Penny lowered the shade. Rick said to her, "So it sounds like the good doctor is helping your sort through things. I thought about getting a Christian counselor, but I am not sure exactly what I believe anymore. Also our human resources department, who gave me a list of recommended counselors whom take our insurance, said to stay away from any psychiatrist or psychologist with any religious affiliation."

The small Bible that Penny sometimes carried with her when she traveled was at the bottom of her purse. She put her right foot next to her purse, touching it from the outside as a surrendering to God, not knowing what to say. She looked back at Howard's seat.

A man standing to his left, touched Howard's shoulder. "Hey, do you want to switch back with me? I'm in 20A by the window," said the man. He was in no way switching seats, but he pointed to Rick. "That was your seat? You three traveling on business? It's like we are playing musical seats!" asked the young man. The woman in the in front of Howard snickered, but he just looked up and pointed again to Rick.

Penny nudged Rick. Rick turned around as the man approached. Rick pulled out his wallet and handed him a hundred dollar bill. Rick apologized for the inconvenience. The man said it was not necessary, but thanked him and went back to his seat.

Penny's returned her hand to his when he said, "This is the thing. You had your friends and Bible study, and I had my work. I was moving in a different direction than you, and it did not make sense to me. I was miserable, and I blamed you. Your idiosyncrasies and eccentricities became a mountain that I looked at every day, knowing that if I got past that mountain, I would find greener pastures, pardon the cliché. I'm not asking. I know you have not figured things out yet."

Penny looked astonished. "Kalli told you! That little"—she paused—"sister of mine." Penny was so angry, but she bit her lip and said nothing more. Her hand stayed on Rick's, although her ego told her to take it back.

Rick laughed. He had enjoyed Kalli's company, and he truly regretted not spending more time with Penny's family, especially since his own family was no longer around. He had grown up with his grandparents, who were quite elderly but had given him a great upbringing in an affluent area. As a boy, Rick had many chores and responsibilities and even though at times he resented the work, his grandparents had been good, godly people that only wanted the best for him.

Rick could not find the words for what he was trying to say, although he had thought long and hard about it. He stayed quiet for a few more minutes and then continued, "Just maybe. Well, let me leave it at this, and then I'll switch seats back with Howard. I am moving to Northern California to take on a new role as CEO of a well-known company. We have not finalized negotiations, but I have verbally accepted the position." Penny removed her hand and stared at him as if he had started speaking a foreign language. "I just would like to see you again after we get off this plane," Rick said, and Penny nodded.

Howard did not know what his chances were, as his intentions were not to be just friends with Penny as they had discussed. Rick had turned around and smiled at him. Howard was more than happy to switch back with Rick, not knowing exactly what Rick and Penny had talked about, but he was sure that Rick wanted back into Penny's life. Howard moved back and greeted Penny.

Just as Penny finished her last cheese and peanut butter cracker, Howard said, "Oh, crackers." He was famished, since he hadn't eaten anything between his previous and current flights. She fetched another pack of crackers out of her bag and offered them to Howard, who readily accepted. He would buy something else later when the flight attendant walked down the aisle. He read the package and commented, "Kosher."

Penny had another bottle of water in her purse, so she handed it to Howard and asked, "Are you Jewish?" When he shook his head, she asked, "Uh, what's your last name?" *Marshall* was the first thing that popped into her mind, perhaps since that was his vocation. "Is it Marshall?" she asked, immediately realizing how dumb and funny that was. "Marshal Marshall," she said quickly. "So what *is* your last name?" His eyebrows went up as he once again shook his head.

Howard took out one of his magazines and said, "Weissman." He showed her his address and name, Howard Weissman. It was a very Jewish spelling of his Hebrew heritage. She howled with laughter. They would be good friends.

Howard chuckled and Penny finally composed herself, a little overly tired she thought to herself. She yawned. Her eyes were watering when she looked up at him again and said, "Do you mind? I am a little tired." She took out her sleep paraphernalia, which included an airline blanket, pillow, and headset. She played Needtobreathe at a low volume as she plugged in her earphones. That was the only Christian group she liked. She also liked a couple of solo artists, such as Laura Duncan, but that was it. Christian music was new to her since her divorce, but she did not tire of it like she did some of her other music.

Howard pulled out his neck my-pillow with the attached hoodie and gave it to Penny, who agreed to try it. Putting the pillow around her neck, she pulled the hoodie over her eyes and head. She loved it. As she positioned herself straight up, he tapped his own shoulder. He was big in stature, and his shoulders were broad. She found his shoulder to be a good resting place for her head as she snuggled up against it. As her eyes closed, hidden to the world beneath the hoodie, Penny fell asleep.

Howard looked down at her covered head smugly, but without conceit. He wished he had met her sooner, but he trusted that however their friendship culminated, it would be a blessing to their lives forever. It would be a long journey, but well worth the pursuit. He put on his sunglasses and closed his eyes as well.

When the plane landed, it was as strange as Penny had expected. Howard retrieved his bag from the overhead compartment, while Rick waited his turn and then did the same. Howard stood in front of Rick to let Penny out. He turned to Rick and told him, in all sincerity, that it had been good to meet him. If Howard was going to get to know Penny, he would want to know Rick, her ex-husband, as well.

On the other hand, Rick did not want to meet any more people associated with Penny. He really wished she had not moved on so quickly. He knew she had not meant to move on, but she was probably just trying to make sense of her life. She could not stay a recluse for too long; she had a life to live. He only wished they had tried harder.

Rick lied and said it had been a pleasure meeting Howard. He realized that he was a little pissed off, not just at Howard but also at Penny, although he knew that was not fair to anyone. Most of all, it was not fair to Penny. Penny waved at Rick after they reached the terminal, and

Howard waited for her while she went to the bathroom. Penny was not sure how to let Howard know that she was being picked up by Rodge, but assumed it did not matter to him.

"So do you need a ride home?" asked Howard. "I parked in short-term parking, so I am not too far from here."

Penny shook her head, reluctant to divulge any more information than he needed to hear. She looked at her wristwatch, which she forgotten to take off during the flight, and hoped that Rick had not noticed it. She loved her watch, but she really did not want Rick to know that she was still holding on to it. "No, Howard, I'm fine. I have a friend picking me up and taking me home, but thanks."

Howard nodded and told Penny that he would text her later, after she got home. Then he headed in the opposition direction from baggage claim, but turned around to make sure Penny was where she needed to be.

Chapter 8

Heaven

Things had changed for Penny at home within the last couple of months. She was not expected back in the office immediately, because she now had work she could do from her humble abode until she had clients again. Penny had not bothered to set her alarm since she had no pending appointments, and she didn't wake up until midmorning.

Her place looked cleaner than when she had left it. There were even a few items in her fridge—a couple of bottles of beer, eggs, a cheese tray, two salads, and some sushi rolls. There was also a coffee cake, ground coffee, a gallon of water, a dark-chocolate bar, and bananas and oranges in a fruit bowl on the counter. Penny loved her boss, but she had never known how much until she arrived home that night. She had never pegged Rodger as domesticated and nice, but now she really did want to get to know him better.

She also had flowers outside her door with a note from Rick, who wanted her to know that he was at a hotel around the corner and available if she wanted company. The note made her smile and roll her eyes at the same time. She placed the flowers in water and put them on the table next to the couch.

Then Penny got dressed for bed, picking out her favorite lightweight pjs decorated with different colored stars. She noticed that the plant in her room was no longer dying. In fact, not only was it thriving, but it also had company, for there were a couple of larger plants by the window. She would have called Rodge that night to thank him, but she was exhausted. He had also just dropped her off, and she figured he was probably still on the road. She texted him thanks and good night, and then slept solid for the next few hours.

At eleven-thirty the next morning, the phone rang and the caller was announced over her Bluetooth device. It was Rodge. She told Bluetooth to pick up as she rushed to grab the cell phone that she had left in the bathroom when she was brushing her teeth the night before. Rodge's voice shouted over the speaker, "Hello?"

Penny grabbed her phone and took him off speaker. Then she retrieved her full cup of coffee from her coffeemaker which was to set to start at 8AM. She took a sip. "Hi, Rodge," she said. "This is really smooth coffee. Isn't it imported from some place in South America?" He told her the coffee beans were from South America, but that he had come across the coffee in a special beanery shop in San Francisco. "I hope you don't mind if I eat and talk at the same time," said Penny.

Penny skipped breakfast except for her cup of joe, but the salads in the fridge were too tempting to pass up. She picked the chopped kale and sunflower salad with a lemon vinaigrette dressing. Kale was not usually her first choice unless it was cooked in broth, but she was so hungry that it was of no consequence.

"No, go ahead," replied Rodger. "I'm headed out, but I just wanted to make sure that you're okay and to ask if you needed anything."

Penny never wanted to seem needy, though she could only think that she must need something, but at last she reluctantly said no. "So where are you headed?" she asked. She should have asked if he was headed to the office, so not to seem like she was into him, but it could have been taken either way. Even though they had grown close with his visits out east, he still kept everything on a professional level, which she respected.

Penny could hear the wind in the background. Then Rodge opened his terrace door, walked inside his apartment, and shut the door behind him. "I'm going to meet Bellamy at a matinee down by the wharf," he said. "It is a film I had not heard of, and unfortunately it's in subtitles, but it has received good reviews."

Penny looked at the clock and wondered if she could make it. Taking another bite of her salad, she tried not to chew and talk at the same time. "Oh yes, Bellamy. I thought you were going to break it off with her. She was too into herself or something like that." She could make it to the wharf if she tried—and if the film didn't start within the next forty-five minutes. "Did you want me to come? I could be that other friend who makes things awkward enough that Bellamy starts to rethink things." Penny was usually passive, but not always.

Rodge snickered and said, "No, Bellamy can handle herself with other people, and she's not so bad. She just doesn't get out much, a little like you. Although she has a lot of friends, she makes work her first priority—except for me." Rodge looked at the clock on his living room wall. "Are you sure that you don't need anything? I'm glad to hear that Kalli is doing better."

Penny still wanted to go and meet him, but she needed to hang back and make other plans. She was disappointed, but not surprised. She once again was reading things into their friendship that were not there. The bleakness of her apartment, except for her flowers, now struck her as lifeless. She thought maybe she could spruce up the place, but she still did not care enough about it. "Maybe we could meet for dinner," she said. She was not sure where the words came from, but there was no taking them back. How desperate she seemed at that moment, but what the heck. Rodge was always so thoughtful, well prepared, and kind.

The doorbell rang. Penny went to the door and opened it slowly, and there stood Dr. Hempstead.

"Hey, I'll let you go. And no, I'm not free for dinner," said Rodge, and he hung up the phone. He was used to women asking him out, and usually he could easily say no. But with Penny, he was sorely tempted to say yes. She seemed so childish most of the time, but there were moments where he felt a connection to her.

Penny looked at her phone sadly, placed it in her pocket, and asked, "To what do I owe this unexpected but delightful visit?" Then she realized that she should have been at his office over twenty minutes ago. She wanted to throw her arms around him, but she didn't want to knock him off balance. "Never mind. Can I get you something to eat or drink?" she asked.

The dear doctor took off his hat and coat and handed them to Penny, who placed them on a stool near the kitchen. "Yes, please," he replied. "That coffee smells good. Maybe add two lumps and some cream?" He did not even think to ask if that was doable. "I just thought we could have our visit here instead of at the office. It does get a little stuffy at times, and since this is one of our extended sessions, this will do just fine." He situated himself on her La-Z-Boy couch. "No, this is not stodgy at all," he said, pleased with his seating arrangement.

Penny looked at her surroundings. *Did he say two lumps?* She opened her fridge and found a small, unopened container of cream beside some milk. She checked the date on the carton, and it was current. She would have never thought to buy cream in a million years, and yet Rodge had. She felt like she lived in a very small world.

She looked in her cabinet for raw sugar, but found only honey. "I have honey, no sugar," she said, but then she spied a small container of Domino sugar cubes on her counter. "Never mind, apparently I have sugar cubes," she said with a laugh. She placed the sugar and cream in serving containers and placed them on a tray with the coffee and a spoon. She also had some coffee cake, compliments of her friend, so she cut them each a slice. "I am so glad I did not miss my appointment. Thank you for coming. I have so much on my mind, and I just did not realize that."

The coffee cup was more of an oversized teacup in a flowered pattern of antique blue and white. Dr. Hempstead lifted it to his lips. "What did you say, Penny? I just want to thank you for the coffee and cake, and for letting me come and visit. I know this part of your journey has been rough." The dear doctor set his coffee back on the tray.

Penny took a seat next to him and took both of his hands. "I have missed you so, dear friend," she said. "I don't know how I have gotten along without you. I really enjoyed our fellowship and letting me share things with you over the phone while I was away, but it is not the same as our walks and talks in person." Penny had softened a bit since she first started her sessions, but her mind was still bent on making things better and not feeling like she was floundering.

The good doctor said nothing. He let her just sit next to him with her hands on his. Somehow she knew that was a moment in time she would come to cherish. It was hard to be still, but she was. Eventually he said that was enough of that, but she did not think so and was close to tears. She could not figure out how he had become such a staple in her life, but she knew it would not last forever. So for the time being, she would just be grateful for his sage advice and company.

Penny told him how Kalli had betrayed her by telling Penny's ex-husband that she was still figuring things out. She asked the good doctor if Kalli had talked with him. He said that she hadn't, but that he expected to hear from her soon since she had left messages with him and they were playing phone tag. After he did make contact with Kalli, he and Penny would no longer be able to talk about her situation so freely since Kalli would be part of their client confidentiality agreement. He then asked Penny if she wanted to talk about Rick, her ex-husband.

The coffee cake on the table was too tempting. Penny would have avoided this conversation with anyone else, but the good doctor perhaps could make sense of what she was feeling. She said, "I don't know what to think or say. He's moving to Northern California, not to be nearer to me, but for a position he is taking with a company." She was trying to make sense of things as she talked with the doctor, but she found it hard. She reached for the coffee cake to deflect, but then she put the piece of coffee cake back down in front of her. "It sounds like he was thrust into dating right off the bat by well-wishers and even professional counsel."

The doctor shook his head and said, "Too much emphasis is put on the here and now, on feeling good for the moment instead of experiencing and even lamenting what's happening when a marriage is devolving and dissolving as yours did."

Penny shook her head too, as if she were an old soul as well. She still could not tell the doctor what she was supposed to do, especially since she could still feel the exhaustion and numbness that went along with their divorce. No, when it came to moving forward, she only knew to take it one breath at time and one step at a time, placing one foot in front of the other.

The cake was now wrapped in a napkin. Penny had understood everything Rick had told her on the plane and she knew that things were still out of focus for him, but she was gaining clarity. "So am I even supposed to date, now that I'm divorced?" she asked. She looked at the doctor perplexed. She had put off asking him that question for a long time, afraid of what the answer might be. "I mean in accordance with what the Bible tells us. I'm not wanting to rush into anything, but I know that Christians do get married more than once. I just want to know what I'm supposed to be focusing on in my life if it's not another person."

The doctor's books were in a bag on the floor beside his feet, and he bent down and picked up the Bible. "The Bible says many things about divorce," he said, "and your conscience should steer the way. Pray, seek God's will, and know that He won't lead you anywhere contrary to what's in the Bible. God never contradicts Himself."

It's so good to be home, Penny thought. It's nice that I really have no one to think about other than myself and my family. Nothing has to be complicated right now. She was fine with not dating, but her thoughts kept going back to Rick. Where was he in the equation? Was she obligated to go back to him? "I still love Rick, but I don't think anything has changed between us. I think we're still miles apart, but if I'm supposed to be with him, maybe I should be okay with dating him again."

The Bible was open to Matthew 19:6–9, which Penny had read previously. But she read it again over the doctor's shoulder as he read it aloud:

6 So they are no longer two, but one flesh. Therefore what God has joined together, let no one separate." 7 "Why then," they asked, "did Moses command that a man give his wife a certificate of divorce and send her away?" 8 Jesus replied, "Moses permitted you to divorce your wives because your hearts were hard. But it was not

this way from the beginning. 9 I tell you that anyone who divorces his wife, except for sexual immorality, and marries another woman commits adultery."

"Divorce is difficult," said the good doctor. "There are right and wrong answers."

Then Penny flipped to 1 Corinthians 7:8-11:

8Now to the unmarried [a] and the widows I say: It is good for them to stay unmarried, as I do. **9**But if they cannot control themselves, they should marry, for it is better to marry than to burn with passion. **10**To the married I give this command (not I, but the Lord): A wife must not separate from her husband. **11**But if she does, she must remain unmarried or else be reconciled to her husband. And a husband must not divorce his wife.

"I read this recently," said Penny. "If I got back with Rick, it would be okay, I guess. But if he does not believe as I do, then I should pray and let the Lord intercede on our behalf until things are better. I am not sure about the details." She did not look up from the Bible as she tried to process her thoughts. "I'm going to be okay being single. It's definitely better than dating, I suppose or even getting back together with Rick right now. He's confused about what people are telling him and what he should be doing."

Dr. Hempstead now squeezed her hand. "There is a lot of confusion in this world." he said, shaking his head.

Penny knew she was guilty of being misled by well-meaning people. Then she told him one of her most embarrassing stories. "I threw up. Remember, I told you. It's everything that makes me anxious and honestly, even the thought of entering into a relationship makes me queasy."

When the doctor asked about other men in her life, Penny said, "I like my male friends as friends, and there is something brotherly about them. But some of my male friends could become more than just friends, but I'm not sure about the future." She looked at the doctor for approval.

The pages of the Bible turned once more as the doctor realized that the change had come. "There's a lot to be said about a lot of things, but most importantly you're asking the right questions and seeking His truths. Stay in fellowship. Other women will be important to you, as you will be important to them. You'll learn a lot from them."

Puzzled, Penny looked at him and asked, "You're not leaving me, are you?" She got up from her seat, rushed to the planner on her desk, and looked at the date. The day's date was circled in red with a note that said, "End of sessions with Dr. Hempstead." She looked back at him, her eyes clouded with tears. "Oh please, doctor, can't we continue and always be friends, like you and Miss Maggie?" She crouched on the floor by his side.

Dr. Hempstead looked at her beseeching eyes, and his eyes teared up too. "It's time for us to move on now. That was our agreement. You are looking in the right direction. I don't have all the answers, but your God does. He is the one who loves you most. Jesus died and rose again and sits at the right hand of the Father interceding for you. He is the Son of God, the Holy One of Israel of the Old Testament, the Promised One. Put your trust in Him."

Penny had to think fast, because she knew that she was not strong enough to continue by herself. "Yes, but where do I look to find out if what you are saying is true?" Her question did not hold water, but she still waited for the answer.

The answer came sweetly, almost as a whisper in her ear: "'Who is he that condemneth? It is Christ that died, yea rather, that is risen again, who is even at the right hand of God, who also make the intercession for us'" (Romans 8:34).

Penny and the good doctor sat on the couch for a while and talked about Jesus, the risen Savior. They looked up various passages in the Bible together, like she had with her mother. They laughed and agreed that the future was not about luck or circumstances, but was being forged in trusting God. The good doctor reassured her that this was the right conclusion for their journey together, she hoped this was not the last time she would see him again.

The Life Of Kalli

Chapter 9

Starting Over

Kalli sat on her bed trying to manage her life from her computer. It wasn't much of a life, she thought, but she knew better than to be negative about her affairs. She would soon lift herself off the bed and into her wheelchair to start her day.

Kalli had once been a gymnast who fought the temptation for coffee on a regular basis, but now she could think of no better way to begin the day than with a cup of joe. It was a brand new life and a brand new day that put her in her brand new wheelchair. She laughed at the positive and negative of her own thoughts. This was going to be a journey, but an ardent one. She considered herself lucky, and the time for feeling sorry for herself had worn thin. Now began the new lease on her life.

The wheels of her chair rolled across the cold wooden floor that she could no longer feel beneath her feet. There were only a few things she was really looking forward to today, and all of them were equally weighted. Her Meals on Wheels was second on her list, after her cup of coffee. She hoped it would be something that suited her appetite. Kalli was not a picky eater, but she hoped for something that was as pleasing to her eye as to her palate. The food would arrive shortly, since she had spent most of her morning in bed and it was nearing noon.

It seemed like a waste of time to spend half the day straining her eyes to peruse her personal finances, among other things, on a small tablet, but Kalli preferred to get that out of the way in the morning so she could have reading time at night. The amount of money she received from her settlement was just a pittance of what she deserved, but her lawyer was not going to fight harder than he had to fight, and she did not care. She figured it would all work out in the end. No faith, no anger, though the remorse lingered. But again Kalli reminded herself that she was through feeling sorry about her circumstances.

The settlement money, along with her insurance, was enough to pay for therapy, a modified vehicle, and savings for future surgeries. She would also have a modest income for life, but she supposed she would never have much to add to her savings account.

Kalli would sock away what she could for her future and be grateful for the money that would supplement the insurance payments for her recovery, which by her own assessment would be minimal. She did not like to think about all the media stories about athletes who come back from their crippled bodies with their 'can do' attitudes. Of course, maybe she had gotten wrong what the doctors had told her, but for now she would just focus on the day ahead.

The third, fourth, and fifth things on her list of activities to look forward to, besides lunch and her first cup of coffee, were therapy, swimming, and dinner with her mother. Mom would bring a tasty, beautifully plated dinner for the two of them, plus there would be leftovers. These events would fill her day, and then her day would end.

★★★

The day eventually passed as Kalli reflected on its events. The Meals on Wheels lunch had been okay, but she probably would not keep the food service for too long, as she expected that she would become more efficient and cook her own meals. She could not help but think of herself as a victim, but if she was also a praying person, that would be the one thing she would pray to God to change—and *fast*, even before her recovery.

The feeling of being needy was loathsome to Kalli, but that's how everyone who came to her door misinterpreted her situation. People wanted her to be handicapped and in need of their comfort and help. They spoke to her as if she would always need their assistance, although she was discovering that she didn't want their help—but for now, that could not be changed. She just could not fall prey to anything that would lead her astray or into self-pity.

The day had gone well, and Kalli had achieved her goals for the day. She was committed to physical therapy and had done her best. Her new therapist, Katie, was a pussy cat—something to cuddle, but good for nothing else, especially six months of sessions. There was just no push or shove. The pain was real, but she wanted more pain and more results. She would call Dr. Mwahl, her surgeon/doctor, in the morning.

Kalli also had set her budget up that morning, called

her investment adviser to see about doing some self-investing through an online institution, and returned phone calls from friends and colleagues. She had not called everyone back yet, but she had gotten to most of them. She felt good about her accomplishment, but not completely satisfied, probably because of the lackluster workout routine with Katie.

Kalli opened her tablet once more and sat down to type. The last thing on her list was to start a story. If she was going to have time on her hands, she wanted something to show for it, and since she was tight on funds, she was limited in what she could do. She had no plan for where to begin except with an outline. Writing was almost surreal and unimaginable for her. She had signed up for a creative writing course in college, but she had ended up dropping it, as she had done with many of her classes.

The night was still young and she really should have stayed the course, thought Kalli, laughing at her pun. She could not remember why she dropped the course, but it had probably been related to people taking their own ideas and the class too seriously. On the other hand, Kalli did not always even need a reason if something felt right. She used to drive her mother crazy when she changed her entire course load by midsemester.

Another thought was that writing would get boring quickly. Kalli remembered that when her professor had explained the course requirements, it had seemed like a lot of work for an elective. She may have even been taking it for an easy grade. That seemed like so many years ago, even though it was actually less than a decade.

Still, it was enough to make her feel old, all of thirty-some years old. If only she had stuck with the course and shown more grit, but that had been true of her entire college experience. Kalli had been free in college, unlike in high school, but in sports, especially gymnastics, she had displayed grit and discipline. She sat, notepad and pen beside her tablet, but nothing came to mind.

Kalli's youth and her golden days of college had come and gone; nevertheless, her entire life until the accident had been good. Now she had more time to reflect on her life decisions, which sometimes was depressing. Before the accident, she'd had a job that paid $120K, she was climbing the ladder quickly, and she spent what little free time she had with friends, fun, and just unadulterated happiness.

Life had been great, despite the fact that it had not prepared her for where she was now. Everyone should be more serious, not so carefree or even careless, but that was not the answer either. Wasn't life supposed to be about the pursuit of happiness, and didn't she do that, even in her whimsical ways? By now Kalli had written a few words on the piece of paper beside her, but then she balled it up and threw it in the trash can. Tears ran down her cheeks, and she roughly wiped them away.

Damn, she thought, *can't I do anything right?* She sat in her chair for the next hour, trying to think of something to write. How could her mind be so empty and yet so full at the same time? This was not writer's block, but more like stage fright. How could she put anything worthwhile down on paper, when she cared about so little? Family, friends, experiences were all a blur in light of her circumstances, but she was not asking much of herself. She just needed to start, and yet there was nothing but a knock on the door.

It was her mother. Kalli was busy, but she could not turn away her own mother. After all, her mom had always been very supportive of Kalli, and now she was excited to spend time with her daughter—and had even brought dinner! Throughout the previous decade, their time together had been limited to holidays and special get-togethers, of which there were usually seven. They had also met for coffee and/or shopping when Kalli had been able to squeeze it into her schedule, but the calls and texts had been unavoidable.

Kalli looked at her computer tablet one last time, where she hadn't even typed a title. She hit a button, and the screen went black. She grabbed the wheels of her chair and started to roll, bumping into the table and spilling sparkling water everywhere. She grunted in anger. "I'll be there in a second, Mom," she said as she grabbed a towel that had been on the floor beside the desk, nearly toppling out of her chair. She laid the towel over the spilled water and left it on the desk. Then she turned and wheeled her way to the door, where her mother was waiting patiently. As Kalli turned the doorknob, the aroma of sage, thyme, and rosemary trickled into her condo.

Her mother said, "Oh, so this is your new place. I love what you have done with everything from the countertops to bamboo flooring. You have great taste for design, and you should think about that. This is bamboo, right?" Placing the food in the retention bag on the counter, she took off her coat and placed it on her own arm.

Kalli instinctively grabbed the coat and laid it across her own lap. "Yes, Mom, it's bamboo. And I had help from a designer and interior decorator with the renovation and the furnishings, but I am glad you think I have potential," she said snarkily. "Dinner smells great. Will you be staying for all of it?" She knew how those words would hit her mother, but she did not care. "It's amazing that I have not had you over before now. It's been two years, and you live only a few miles from here." Had Kalli been able to do finish everything on her list for the day, she might have been in a better mood. But as it was, she just wanted to eat, read, take her pain medication, and sleep. She would start again tomorrow.

The two sat quietly at the small table in Kalli's kitchen by the window. She had cracked open the sliding glass door to let in a slight breeze. Kalli did not want to sit in a regular chair; the wheelchair was more secure and supportive for now. She was famished, since her workout had left her tired and hungry. She lifted her fork filled with mashed potatoes, something she normally would not eat.

"Can we pray first, Kalli?" asked her mother, who already had her hands folded in her lap. Her head was bowed, and she was afraid to look up at her daughter, whose temper she suspected was about to flare. Kalli could not catch her mother's eyes to ask, *How dare you?* So she just muttered for her to go ahead.

Kalli's mom prayed a simple prayer to bless the food and thank God for His provision. As soon as the amen was uttered, Kalli once again lifted her fork to her mouth. She ate and ate and ate more. Her mother's mouth and eyes were wide open as she tried not to stare, but she was unmistakably surprised and asked, "Are you too full for dinner? I mean, from dinner. I mean, are you too full for dessert?"

Kalli looked at her mother through teary eyes and smiled. Dessert was just what she needed, so she nodded vigorously. Then she wiped her mouth and nose, which was now running from the spicy Pecanha steak, a piece of sirloin cap her mother had kindly picked up from Kalli's favorite Brazilian steak house.

"I made hasselback apples with pecan streusel and whipped mascarpone," said her mother. "It's filling, if you would rather wait." The casserole she had made to be eaten at a later date was still sitting on the counter, and she wished she had placed it in the refrigerator.

Kalli proudly looked at the table, where most of her mother's dishes sat half empty. "Bring it on!" she said, now in a much better mood.

Quickly her mother was up and plating the apples on the dessert dishes, adding mascarpone on top. Then she grabbed the casserole and set it in the back of the refrigerator, where it was easily seen since there was nothing in front of it. Walking back to the table, she asked, "Would you like me to pick up some groceries for you tomorrow?" Then she placed the dessert plates on the table and took a seat.

Normally that question would have put Kalli in a mood again, but she had dessert in front of her and it was a good day, despite her lack of accomplishment. "Sure, if you would not mind. I think I have only yogurt, dried fruit, and a banana in the fridge, and two out of those three probably don't belong in there. Other than that, it's just energy drinks, which I don't need since all I do is sit on my ass, and I have flavored water." Kalli thought about it, and her mom's suggestion was not as irritating as she had first thought. "I was going to order delivery, and they put everything away for me since it's part of the delivery fee. But if you were bringing me dinner anyway, what are a few groceries, right?" Kalli established firm eye contact with her mother.

Her mother just smiled and placed her napkin back on her lap.

Kalli looked at her, thinking maybe she was missing something. *Is a thank-you in order? What does she want from me? Isn't it time for her to leave?* She tried not to look impatient. She could tell her mother was praying, so she waited for her to look up and then pointed to her own watch.

Her mother laughed, which did not sit well with Kalli, and said, "I'm not leaving yet." She wished that she could rewind all the time she had spent with her two beautiful daughters and son, and relive the years that she was married to "that man," as she had often endearingly referred to him. Life should not be taken for granted—not one minute of it. She should have treasured every time her children called her Mom, every "I love you" she heard over the phone, and even every dirty diaper she changed. *Well, that might be overkill*, she thought, but she missed having her family close. The one thing she knew for sure was that she should have been more grateful.

As her mother raised her fork, almost like a toast, Kalli looked down at her food and started eating. "So do you pray before dessert too?" she asked. "By the way, this is really good. Thank you." There, she said it.

Puzzled, her mom replied, "No, I was just praying to be praying. You caught me? It's good for me to lift up the things that bother me, or just to say thanks. Kalli, you are one of my biggest blessings. All of my children are blessings. Don't you say prayers of thanks?"

Now it was Kalli's turn to be a little puzzled. "Thanks for *what*? Never mind. Thank you for the food. It changed my day from rotten to okay. I really appreciate you stopping by tonight, even though you interrupted my work." The plates on the table needed to be cleared, but they could wait until tomorrow—if she would just leave.

The plate of roasted vegetables seasoned with rosemary and thyme once again started to look appetizing. Before Kalli's accident, that would have been the only thing she ate, along with perhaps an ounce of her favorite steak, but now she was abnormally hungry. She finished her hasselback apples and started for the vegetables.

"You know, I think you should see a psychiatrist. He could prescribe you some anti-depressants. Also there may be a different counselor who could talk with you more regularly." her mom said gingerly. She waited for Kalli's reply, hoping that her daughter had already realized that sometimes you cannot talk through depression.

Kalli's reply was soft-spoken as well. "I'm not depressed. I'm sad for a reason. There's a difference. I'm glad that you still want to play mom, but I'm a big girl and have been for some time. So I might not get around as much, but I'll figure it out. Depression medication is for people who may have a reason to be depressed—or not, but they can't go forward with doing harm to themselves or to others in some way. In other words, it's hard for them to cope with where they are in life with others or themselves. That is not me. I'm hanging in there and trying to move forward. It won't come in a day or a month or even a year, but I'll get to where I'm supposed to be," she said as gracefully as she could. She was hoping that her mom would look relieved, but instead Kalli saw what she hated the most.

The pity in her mom's eyes oozed out in her words. "Kalli, I know this is not easy. I'm just saying that if you need medication to take the edge off for just a little while, until you figure this out, it doesn't make you a weaker person. Maybe you could also try your sister's counselor. She is making great strides with him."

The persistence was wearing on Kalli's nerves. "Mom, I'm on minimal pain medication, which I'll be done with in a month, and that's all I need to take the edge off. That's for the pain that I feel every time I move in the wrong direction. I know what you're thinking, that my counselor is not the best in the world, but the 'dear doctor,' as my sister calls him, sounds awful. He's super-old and totally out of touch, besides being deep into religion. My sister is naive and needs someone to tell her what to think. You should worry about her cultish behavior. That is not me."

In her purse, Kalli's mother had a book about trusting God, and she had been thinking of passing it on to Kalli. But now she felt like it wasn't the right time, and probably she should hold on to it for a little longer. "I am trying to understand." she told Kalli.

Kalli continued to explain her thoughts. "I need someone to help me think and sort through things. My guy, my counselor, is shrewd and runs his own company on the side. He's also published and frequently written up in journals. I saw him regularly for the first few months, but now it's less often. He sees through the normal BS, and I check in with him every few weeks so it does not get strange between us. Remember, it's been six months now, and this is the first time I've been on my own in my own condo. I can do this—I just need time. You get it." But once again, Kalli saw something that angered her.

The worried expression on her mother's face was worth a thousand words. Kalli's mother didn't need to say anything, but she did anyway. "Kalli, I'm proud of you, and you have come a long way, but I believe you're depressed. I'm not doubting that your judgment is sound, but I think you should at least talk with someone on a weekly basis who knows better."

The ice maker in the refrigerator turned on, and Kalli's mom jumped. Kalli was mad. She did not get her mother. Hadn't Kalli been through enough? "Did that startle you?" Kalli asked. "Because this will startle you more. Mom, people who have gone to war and dealt with two sets of rights and wrongs are going to have something to deal with mentally."

The dishes in front of her were tempting, but Kalli's mother wanted to concentrate on what her daughter was saying. "That's true," she said, hoping that Kalli would become less offended as their conversation continued.

Kalli pushed the dish in front of her in her mother's direction as she leaned toward the table. "They may need depression medication because they have issues and situations that they need to backtrack, figure out and for which to come to terms. On the other hand, you have me. I know what my situation is, and I have no moral issues or anything that goes against my conscience. What I have to deal with is plain vanilla, my handicap."

Kalli's mother was interested in what her daughter was expressing. And as long as Kalli was able to communicate her own thoughts, she didn't feel contempt for her mother. "Keep talking," said her mother.

Kallie saw some vegetables that she could nipple on, but she had lost the desire. "Medication will not take my problem away. It might turn it a lighter color for a while, but the root cause will still be there. That's what I'm working on, without any medication except my pain meds. When that root cause goes away, I'll see more clearly. If I need an antidepressant, then I'll talk with someone. I am sad, and I'll continue to be sad for a long while, but I won't let that define me." Kalli now felt like she was in a safe space.

Her mother smiled sweetly and longed for the days when she had walked Kalli to school, hand in hand. Their discussions had been kinder and longer then. "Kalli, you have a good point," she said.

"It might surprise you to learn that I *did* talk with the 'good doctor.' That's how I know that he is deep into religion. That was his advice, his assessment, even though I lied and did not want to tell you. People have problems, and unless we address those problems, we're only treating the symptom," said Kalli, who was starting to cry.

Her mom's "I told you so" expression was written all

over her face. She got up and started to clear the dishes from the kitchen table. The first plate she grabbed was the roasted vegetables that Kalli had occasionally continued to eat. She was quiet for a while, but then she said, "I think the good doctor is wrong. You are clearly upset and not yourself."

The wheelchair started to move backward. Kalli wheeled herself into the living room and turned on the TV. She announced the show that she wanted to watch, and it loaded. She picked the only show she knew her mother hated, *The Big Bang Theory*. Passive aggressive, she knew. She had words, but she wanted to sleep well tonight. Still, her mother's words resonated within her like an echo in a canyon. She paused the show and turned her chair toward her mother.

Here it comes, Kalli's mother thought. She needed something to protect her throat, but it was too late for that.

Kalli said, "I think you had better leave now. I'll do my own damn dishes. By the way, have you ever thought that *you* may need counseling? After all, we don't keep in touch with you. Your children don't like you. It's always you reaching out to us. Coby, your all-American son, serves in the army, reaches out to the homeless, is part of the community, always doing and giving for and to others, but he doesn't have time to talk with you, or so you say. Yet he calls me, and now he's talking with Penelope. And what about Penelope, who swore off all of us for the longest time? She talks to me on a regular basis. So Mom, what's wrong with you?"

There was more, her mother assumed. Continuing

to wash the dishes, she said, "I talk to them both, Kalli. I wish I had more quality time with them, but I understand that their lives are complicated." That was information that Kalli could use against her for the moment. The sound of dishes clanking together got a little louder.

Kalli said, "If you're taking depression medication—and I assume you are—I'd double it. That is, since your problem, no time—oops, no *quality* time—won't be going away anytime soon. I wouldn't stop taking it, even if a doctor told you to, if I were the unloved you."

Kalli waited, but her mother recanted nothing. There was only the sound of silence, no dishes clanking. "I think that's enough, Kalli," said her mother.

Kalli had her mother's undivided attention, and she wasn't finished. "You and the horse you rode in on need to leave. Oh, what's that you say? You don't have anything between your legs, and that goes for your ears too? I guess that's also part of your problem, so you'd better medicate."

The sigh from her mother's lips was deep and woeful. "You are a wicked girl, Kalli." There were no tears on her mother's face, but she was visibly shaking. Not only did Kalli not care, but she was pleased. "I will pray for you," said her mom, retrieving her coat from the couch where Kalli had placed it. She almost made it to the door, but then stopped to look around for anything she might have left. She went to the counter and picked up the bags in which she had brought the food. "Bye, Kalli," she said.

Kalli smiled smugly and switched the television back on. "Wicked me. Yes, do pray. After all, you never prayed for me before, and look where I am today. I'm sure your prayers will be heard and I will be a changed woman, able to walk again." There it was, the cold hard truth. She did not blame God, if there was one, but her mom should.

Kalli simply was where she was, and she needed support and guidance from other people to help her keep moving forward and not get stuck, but her mom was trying to drive a nail into her coffin. Kalli did not want to be dead on the inside and be forced to accept it. She wanted to know and feel the pain to which she was entitled; her pain was there for a reason. She was resolved not to be sad and to fight her way through it, but why did her mother want everything to be okay when things were *not* okay? Why did she want to placate and control every situation? Why did her father have to leave her alone? Kalli started to tear up, but she would not look at her mother.

Her mother put her hand on Kalli's shoulder and asked, "Are you going to be all right? I can stay over if you want."

Kalli looked up at her in disbelief and switched off the television.

"You aren't wicked, but you have a snake's tongue—and you owe me an apology," her mother said. "Also, I get the medication deal. I'm sorry for trying to push something on you that you don't need. I just don't know how to handle your situation."

Kalli turned her wheelchair just enough to hug her mother around her waist. "I know, Mom, and I am sorry. I'm just trying to get through this. We all love you, and I'm glad Penelope is talking with you again. You can be a bit much, but it must have been hard being a single mom for all those years. At least, that's what we tell each other."

Her mom laughed and said, "So that's my excuse for being a bit much? I was a single mom after you kids were all grown up? Okay … It's okay, we're all moving forward." She bent over and kissed Kalli's forehead. "You're a good girl, and you'll find your way. I know you will. By the way, Coby is coming over tomorrow to visit. Text him your schedule so he knows what's good for you." Kalli did not see her Mom take a book out of her purse and place it on the coffee table. Her mom then left the condo; she shook her head and inhaled deeply.

Chapter 10

Coby

The condo door was slightly opened to the hallway when Coby came to visit. Coby peeked his head inside and looked around. "Kalli, are you home?" He came in and shut the door behind him.

The patio door was open, and Kalli was sitting outside drinking a sparkling water and eating yogurt. She removed her earpods and yelled, "I'm out on the patio." Then she put her pods back in and turned the volume low.

The refrigerator door was ajar slightly and had been beeping, but apparently Kalli had not heard it from outside. Coby opened it the rest of the way and put some food into the fridge. He took out his mom's casserole, cut himself a piece, and placed in on a plate. He covered the dish back up and put it back in the refrigerator, a little taken aback with the lack of food. He grabbed the bag he had on the counter and headed out to the patio.

The bird feeder outside the patio was empty. *Need to remember birdseed*, Coby said under his breath as he took out his phone and made a note. Then he took a good look around, and everything appeared to be in order, tidy and clean. He was specifically looking for anything that would help or hinder accessibility for Kalli.

Coby put his arms around Kalli's shoulders. "Hi, sis. It's nice out here." He put the brown bag on the far end of the patio table. "I brought orange juice, croissants and a breakfast sandwich with gouda, egg, and bacon. Anything else, you might need?" Kalli was the baby of the family and she was coddled by all, including Coby.

Kalli shook her head and reached for the bag. "I assume you've talked with mom. Did she say anything? I gave her a hard time, but she did not leave crying. So I'll have one of those croissants if you will pass the bag, and whatever you're holding looks good too. Is that Mom's casserole?"

Coby slid the plate of her mom's famous vegetable, meat, and pasta casserole across the table. "I did stop at Mom's this morning and she did not say anything about it. I am going to get myself some more casserole."

Kalli's mouth was full of croissant. "So did she give me more food? She is suppose to bring by groceries later. So Mom didn't say anything?"

Coby shook his head. "Not a word, other than you were good for company and probably would appreciate some food." he replied. "She loaded me up with staples, like milk, ketchup, mustard, mayo, pickles, and the like. I put everything she gave me into the refrigerator. She is a good woman."

The casserole on Kalli's plate was already half eaten. "I know she is.", she said while perusing her notes written on a piece of paper for the start of her book. She felt a little guilty, but was glad she did not have to elaborate on their disagreement. She reached across and opened the brown bag, pulled out another croissant and the sandwich, and added them next to her plate. She was happy. "Go ahead, just leave me enough for a couple of meals." Kalli really did not want to part with any of her casserole, but Coby was her brother, and she loved him.

Coby watched as Kalli devoured her food and then excused himself from the table. He hoped his little sister would be able to work it off in physical therapy, but he strongly doubted it. Since she had just been released from the hospital, the therapist should start her off slow and at low impact, not high impact. Coby thought about how he could bring low-fat food, instead of what she was eating now, but he guessed that Kalli would have none of it.

The refrigerator door was ajar and beeping again. Coby looked it over and adjusted part of the door seal back into place. He would bring something to fasten it if the problem reappeared. He plated himself another piece of casserole and grabbed a water bottle. "Hey," he yelled from the kitchen, "I didn't come over just to bring you goodies and shoot the breeze. I need to know if you're interested in helping out with one of our programs for city youth."

He walked back to the table with a piece of casserole twice the size of his first one. As he sat down, Kalli glared at his plate, but Coby didn't notice. But when she grabbed the sparkling water from his hand and set it next to her food, he thought, *Are you kidding? Didn't I just ask if she needed something?*

Kalli said, "I'm not sure. It seems like it could be a lot."

Coby returned to the kitchen, where the refrigerator was *not* chirping this time. He grabbed another water and shut the door firmly. "Okay, then," he said as he walked back outside. "I need your commitment. It's not overly taxing, but it does require effort. You'd be hosting about seven kids between the ages of seven to twelve for about two hours in the afternoon."

Kalli looked up, surprised. Suddenly her apartment felt small. "Are you sure?" she asked.

Coby turned, looked closely at his sister's living space, and said with a confident tone, "This is perfect. If it's nice out, they can sit right there on the lawn with cushions and blankets. You will be reading stories and feeding them lunch that we provide. We just don't have any other place for them to go. It would only be twice a week, but it could lead to other things if you are interested."

Kalli's napkin fell to the ground beside her chair, but Coby quickly snatched it up and placed it back on the table. Unsure what to think about his proposal, she said, "No, I'm not interested in other things, although I don't mind helping out when needed. I can help the project until the recreation center is completed." Looking around for something else to eat, she spotted Coby's dish with only a fourth of the casserole left.

Coby's mouth was full, but sizing up his sister's threatening appetite, he swallowed hard and stuffed a huge piece of his casserole into his mouth. He needed to finish talking, but that could wait for a moment. First he chased the food down with some sparkling water, and then said, "One other young adult will be coming by as well, since we mandate two adults, one staff, and one civilian. We don't have a place for these kids during that time slot at the center, so I really appreciate what you are doing."

As expected, his sister reached for his plate and the last of the casserole. She crammed a forkful of food into her mouth, which she did not bother to shut before speaking. Coby was a little grossed out and wondered where his well-mannered dainty sister had gone. "I will look forward to it," Kalli said, "since I don't have anything else to do." Coby wasn't sure if he understood her correctly, but he nodded in agreement.

Coby stayed and chatted for a while until it was time to go. Then he offered to drive Kalli to therapy, but her pickup had already been arranged by the center. He thought about how great it was that Kalli lived in a coveted first-floor condo with access to the outside. Then he said a prayer of thanksgiving that his sister was still with them and that God was still providing for them.

Kalli was glad for her new commitment, but she wondered if it would be too much. Lunch and reading sounded pretty easy, but since the children were a little older, it might make it more interesting for them if their time together was more interactive. She was not sure of the material she would be working with yet, but she would figure it out.

★★★

The driver knocked on the door of her condo, and she opened it wide. "Ready?" he asked. She smiled and rolled through the door as he held it open and then closed it behind her. "May I?" he asked, taking hold of the handles at the back of her wheelchair. But Kalli wanted to do everything by herself until she was totally comfortable, so she just said no.

Kalli wondered who her new therapist would be and hoped that she would not be as lax as Katie, her previous therapist. She wondered how much training the therapists had and who wrote the material for their workouts, because most of it looked standard. If someone could create exercises and routines specific to her needs, that would be ideal, but perhaps she was thinking too much about it. She hoped that other clients who worked with Katie would not resent her, but better that than having things go south or feeling angry.

Katie was at the door when Kalli entered the medical training center, but Kalli said, "I'm with another therapist today. Sorry for the inconvenience."

Katie just laughed. She had a good disposition with people, but laughing at her clients would not fall in that category.

Kalli said, "I talked with my doctor, who said he would have me reassigned. He even offered to transfer me to a facility closer to my house, but I told him that any facility good enough for my favorite football team is good for me. He laughed at that." Kalli usually did not talk much, but she found it hard to resist since she had decided to take her pain medication before her workout.

The receptionist at the front desk interrupted her and said, "Hi, Kalli. I'm signing you in with Katie again today. We couldn't schedule you with your new therapist, Christina, until next week."

The radio was playing Katie's favorite song, "The Thunder Rolls," an older song by Garth Brooks. She was singing happily, and Kalli realized that Katie had an amazing voice, but still wasn't pleased.

Katie said, "Kalli, I'll push you a little harder today to make up for yesterday, but you have to realize that there's method to our madness. It's not like a routine that you just go and do. We need to figure out what works and what doesn't. Everything's connected, so it's not as easy as just exercising and stretching. If we want to build muscle around certain nerves to decrease pain, so that you can get off your meds with less effort, we need to consider this. Also, in some areas where we already know there's nerve and muscle damage, we need to work only with specific muscles rather than other muscles that might be torn or otherwise damaged. We have to be careful and take it slowly, working on some areas only slightly and other areas harder."

A big red ball was placed in Kalli's lap. *Like I can do anything with this*, she thought.

Christina held out her hand, which Kalli accepted by reaching her arm over the top of the large ball. "I'm Christina, and I design some of the routines and specific exercises. I've been working hard on yours, and we will be continually critiquing what works and what doesn't. I know your expectations are high, but we'll exceed them. You're in good hands with any of our therapists. I would have introduced myself to you yesterday, but I was picking out wedding dresses."

The gym seemed bigger to Kalli today as she looked around. She had lost interest in their conversation when Christina mentioned wedding dresses. The gym had more equipment, or maybe they had just moved it around.

"Really?" she said. She would still accept Christina as her new therapist since Christina seemed to have the most tenure, but she also realized that Katie was proficient and that she, Kalli, had made a mistake. "I am looking forward to working with you next week, Christina," she said. Christina and Katie exchanged looks. Then Kalli asked, "When is the wedding?"

The red ball was handed to another woman who needed it to do her exercises. She placed it between her back and the wall, several feet from where they were standing, and started doing squats.

"Three weeks from now," replied Christina, "and then I will be gone for the next two weeks." She readjusted the ball behind the woman's back, for which the woman thanked her—even though it obviously made the squats more difficult. "During that time, Katie will take as many of my patients as possible. Are you sure you want to switch to me before I go on leave?" The woman counted to four, watching herself in the mirror as she started to rise. Christina also watched her as she reached five of ten squats.

Kalli said, "I'll let you know, since you'll be with me for only a week. I'm assuming you're taking time off before the wedding as well, but yes, that would be acceptable. Just don't expect me to change my mind."

Katie did not say anything, but she was not pleased. They did not always let clients switch unless they were insistent, and certainly not to Christina or Mike, who were usually reserved for the professional athletes. Katie thought that Kalli must have an inside connection, but she could not figure out who it was.

"I guess we are going to run five minutes over since I was here on time," said Kalli.

The woman doing the squats reached her target of ten. Christina waved as she walked across the floor to her client. Kalli was upset that she did not have Christina today as her therapist. Katie cheerfully said "Follow me" and waved her arm forward as if she was a Disney princess in a parade. Kalli wheeled her chair over to a small corner of the medical training center.

The van driver picked Kalli up promptly at the end of her session. She finished five minutes early since she did not want an ice treatment at the end of her session. It was optional, and she had an ice machine at home to use if necessary.

The driver took Kalli straight to her building and helped her into her condo. He gave her his business card, which said, "Fred Catchem, Licensed Special Driver" with the name of the company, and explained that she could ask for him in particular.

Oh please, she thought, *special driver because I am special.* But he did drive smoothly with no quick stops. "I might request you. Thank you for the card," she said.

Once inside, Kalli realized how alone she was. There was no talking in the background and no one with whom she could strike up a conversation. This was going to be an adjustment for her. Her mainstay had been working, and now she had a lot of alone time on her hands.

Kalli was employed by a consulting firm in the city, and they had heavily relied on her knowledge and expertise in communications, which had kept her working overtime. But since the accident, she needed to take time off for recovery. Unfortunately even if she wanted to go back, she could not return to that same job. They had told her that they needed to hire someone to replace her, but they offered to create a new position for Kalli if and when she decided to come back. Her feelings were hurt, but she had already made the call and would stick with it.

The fan in her condo was blowing full strength, which was odd since she hadn't left it on. At first she wondered who might have let themselves in, but then she realized quickly that she was still alone. When he had closed the door, the driver must have accidentally hit the switch that turned on the fan. That fan had two switches, including one on the other side of the room, which Kalli turned off.

Kalli's heart was beating fast. The fan being on made her think about her safety and living on the first floor. She had never worried before, since she had been more agile than most people and was hardly ever home, but now she felt vulnerable. She would see if Coby knew of an inexpensive but reputable company to install a security system.

A slight breeze was still blowing into the room. Kalli went to the patio door, which was slightly open. *Now that is truly odd*, she thought. She went outside, where the cool breeze made her feel free. She could see people walking, which brought her a feeling of comfort. She looked down and saw a single cigarette butt on the grass at the edge of her patio. She turned her head and looked back inside her dark apartment. She did not want to be a coward, to panic and call the police, but she felt safer outside.

Her purse was hanging on the edge of her chair, so

Kalli pulled out her phone and texted her mother: "Are you on your way over?"

"Yes," her mother texted back, "but I'm stopping to get groceries first. I thought I would cook dinner for us at the apartment."

"How long?" asked Kalli's next text.

"Not too long," texted her mother. "Is everything okay?"

The phone rang, and Kalli picked up without saying hello. "Everything is okay. I'm just hungry. Can you forget the shopping? Come on over and we'll order in tonight? Also, thanks for the ketchup and shit. Coby dropped it off this morning." She knew her mom would freak out at the profanity.

"It's not much of a thanks when you use profanity," said her mother. "I'll be there shortly."

Inside of twenty minutes, the doorbell rang and Kalli answered it. Her mother was wearing a light jacket, which she took off after setting down a bag of items for the kitchen. But instead of taking the jacket from her mother, Kalli said, "You can put your jacket in the bedroom if you like."

Her mom stepped to the coat closet directly behind her and opened the door. "Well, I can also hang it in here, can't I?" Laughing, she went back to the kitchen and unloaded the kitchen utensils and other things that she had picked up for Kalli's apartment earlier.

Quiet for a moment, Kalli said, "Well, I think I left my sweater on the edge of my bed. Do you mind getting it for me? If it's not on the bed, it might be underneath—or hanging in the back of my closet, if you don't mind looking for it."

Kalli's mother looked at her oddly. "Sure, just let me finish putting these things away. I thought you were trying to do everything for yourself these days. But I don't mind doing your errands or looking for your sweater. Just keep in mind your goal."

Kalli turned on the television and waited for her mom to finish putting things away. "Do you mind that I turned on the television?" she asked sweetly, gazing intently at the flat screen.

The spatulas, tongs, and a wooden spoon now found a home on the counter, along with other kitchen essentials, in a tarnished tin that perfectly matched the kitchen backsplash. Pleased, Kalli's mom put her hands on her hips. She had redecorated the kitchen with knickknacks that had meaning for a cook. "Sweet of you to ask me this time, Kalli. Did you already order dinner?"

Kalli's phone buzzed with a text message. "What's that? No, I wasn't sure what you wanted." Distracted, she said, "Never mind about the sweater."

The doorbell rang, the door opened, and Coby walked in with a smile on his face. "Thanks, Kalli, for letting me come over. I know it was last minute, but I heard Mom's cooking, and this is a lot closer than her house out in the sticks." He walked over to his mom, put his arm around her, kissed her on the cheek, and said, "Hi, Mom."

His mom was pleasantly surprised and immediately envisioned future family dinners at Kalli's house, but the grin on her face didn't last long.

Kalli turned off the television and said, "Um, Coby,

could you check my bedroom for an intruder—whom I'm pretty sure does not exist. Look under my bed, in my closet, and in the bathroom behind the shower curtain." She glanced over to see her mother's expression—big eyes and an open mouth. Coby checked the bedroom and came back out before any further words were spoken.

Kalli's mom put her hands on her hips and said, "Really, Kalli? Do you not like me just a little more than that?"

Coby looked at her sister's blank expression. There was a loud bang outside, but everyone ignored it. "What, Kalli, did you ask her to go in and look for something? What's wrong with you? She's our mom. Why did you think someone might have been in here anyway?"

Kalli turned the television back on, but she turned the volume down. "The fan was on, the patio door was open, and a cigarette butt was on the grass next to the patio. Mom, I was going to be right behind you. It would have been you and me together, and then I wouldn't have felt so stupid if there had been no intruder. And if there *had* been an intruder, they might have gotten you first, but they definitely would have eventually gotten me as well."

A bit perplexed, Coby and his mother looked at each other with raised eyebrows.

Kalli abruptly turned her chair and rolled toward her mother. "Sorry, Mom," she said. "I wasn't sure anyone was in there."

Coby and their mother knelt beside her, and Mom said, "Kalli, it's okay. You need to know that even if you're afraid, you're not alone. Many people, including us, feel scared and vulnerable, but this is a season in your life where you need to get help. You need to talk through your fears with a professional, whether it's your busy and notable psychologist or Penny's aged and wise 'dear doctor.' It might be easier to get in touch with Penny's doctor, and he might give you a break on the cost and work better with the allotted number of sessions within your insurance guidelines."

Kalli looked at her mother and brother, not knowing what to think—except that her life had changed so much.

Then it was Coby's turn. "Do you know what *Unus Pro Omnibus, Omnes Pro Uno* means?"

It was a rhetorical question, but Kalli interrupted him. Already bored with the conversation, but sorry for her lack of judgment she answered. "Yes, I believe it was on *The Truman Show.* The town motto was 'One for all, and all for one.'"

Coby turned her chair directly toward him and said, "Okay, the words are the same but I was going in a different direction. Even the three musketeers would have been a better choice, but that is us now. In the military, we have to have each other's backs, so we are committed to everyone as a whole. We don't single out any individual as more valuable than any other; we just work together. That is what a family should look like too. We don't leave anyone behind, or in your case, push anyone in front! I know this isn't you right now; in fact, right now this is not any of us. We are going to get through this if we …" He paused and tried to gather his emotions.

Mom grabbed Coby's hand and squeezed. She was proud of him. Typically, on any given holiday, he would have ripped into his little sister for her selfishness and lack of compassion for others.

Kalli said, "Don't say it. Don't say it. If we trust in God." Her brother looked at her mother, who looked back at him. He shrugged, and she shrugged back. Kalli said, "No, come on. That's what you were going to say, isn't it? Something about God and a bigger perspective?" Kalli swiveled her chair around to face her mother.

"So what's for dinner, Mom? Kidding, Mom texted and said you were ordering in for dinner.", said Coby.

As much as Kalli hated to admit it, she did not mind having the company for dinner. Her fast-paced life had left gaps that were filling in quickly.

The refrigerator was not as empty as it had been the previous day, but still Mom would not be able to muster up dinner. Kalli looked at her phone and said, "We have a variety of options." She rattled off her top three choices, the first two of which could be there within minutes.

Chapter 11

Could It Be Me?

Coby was stationed in Beirut. It had been three weeks since he had last seen his sister, and he was wondering if she was okay. An image flashed across his screen, and all thoughts of family were erased. This base usually did not stage drills, either regular or irregular, because it was too small. It was satellite intel that moved him closer to his display. Several fighter jets crossed over into international waters. *Not a drill*, he thought, *but where?*

He checked the satellite imagery on other screens as he typed in various codes to see if he could pick up something nearby. Something that would warrant a warning shot or a flyby. He strained his eyes, but he could not see anything. His commander in chief was now looking over his shoulder. He was looking hard, but he saw nothing.

The activity on the first screen jumped. "What are we looking at, Lieutenant Marshall?" asked Colonel Anderson.

"Sir, I am not completely sure, but it looks like something is headed our way," replied Coby. "It's unusual to see anything launched from this base. It is one of our covert bases that we prefer to keep hidden, and if we do launch anything, we jam the signal. This time I can see it in plain view, which means so can everyone else."

Colonel Anderson leaned closer into the screen. He was waiting for someone to pick up on the other end of the phone that he held to his ear. "Whoever the hell I'm speaking to, get Lieutenant Colonel Johnson on the phone," he said. Looking at the screen, he was not alarmed by what he saw except for the breach of protocol. "This mistake is over the top, and it's too late to be rectified."

Then the planes vanished off screen, and Colonel Anderson asked, "What's the problem here? We are not picking up any communications across screen to tell us this is ours. And what the hell are we looking at in international waters? How the hell do you expect operations to do its job if they don't know it's a drill? We are exposed. Nobody radioed it in, it was not scheduled, and you did not cut the feed until now. Don't think this is going unpunished. If it was up to me, you would be demoted." He hung up the phone. His face was fire red as he slowly walked away from Coby's station.

Coby did not turn around to study the colonel, but he figured this was not just a small military base near Beirut. Colonel Anderson pulled up his phone and looked at Coby's profile. He walked over to the coffeepot, which sat next to the more modern machines that required a person to select and insert a pod. *Too much trouble for a cup of joe*, he thought. He poured himself a cup of coffee that resembled black tar. He was the only person who poured from that pot; everyone else used the more modern method of making coffee, but they all knew better than to disturb his unconventional method of brewing.

Colonel Anderson needed a bigger screen to study Coby Marshall's background, but he was still too mad to sit in the comfort of his office. He walked down the hall to yell at someone who should have picked up the intelligence from a different source. As he walked and sipped his hot coffee, he got more angry. Heads would roll, but not his. They would have to move the satellite base somewhere else nearby and keep it hidden. It would be an impossible feat, and the rest of the world would be waiting for it.

Thinking like that was above Coby's pay grade. He was just glad he had caught it. He liked it when things made sense, and when they did not, he went into overdrive seeking answers. Fixing some things was within the parameters of his abilities, but most were not.

★★★

The small condo was filled with eight children and two adults. Kalli's demeanor had not changed much. She was stiff and only a little comfortable around the children. Sadie, who usually accompanied the children, was less like Mary Poppins and more like the fun sister. She complained when lunch did not arrive soon enough, and she was always looking at her phone. Kalli realized that she, Kalli, was the grown-up in the group and that she liked adults better than kids.

The book, *Out of the Hidden Darkness*, was incredibly interesting. Kalli loved to read, but most books that she read were a little drier, not kids' books. She usually selected books that were based on real life or from some "must read" list, which kept her current, but this was pure fiction.

Out of the Hidden Darkness was about a king who was to be married to a duchess with whom he was pleased, but he fell into a trance and followed a powerful queen into the dark forest. They were at the part in the book where the king started to become aware that he was in a trance. He wanted to go home, but there was no one to help him wake up. The queen had kept her eye on him forever and would soon be married to him. A search party was on its way, but it would be impossible for them to find him in time, since the way was hidden to anyone who was in the light.

Kalli was a fast reader, and the children were always asking her to read more slowly. She had thought about making the experience more interactive and having the children role-play different scenes, but that was before she became interested in the ending. She decided she would do something more entertaining for the next book, since she would have that reading material ahead of time and thus could do more planning.

Kalli began reading: "'The young brigade was under instruction to find the King no matter how tough it got, but they were not to leave each other alone or split up. They were stronger as one, but they were getting frustrated since they could not find their way.' Oh no, what do you think is going to happen?" she asked the children. She looked over the young faces and imagined them as the young brigade. *What the heck*, she thought, and called them by characters' names instead of their real names. "Yes, Chaucer?" said Kalli.

Seven-year-old Ellie laughed and said, "Well ..." She was the youngest in the bunch and the most inquisitive. She used a British accent that sounded more Australian than British, which made sense since her mother was dating someone from Australia. "Well, I think I will lead my young brigade back home and wait for the king there ... since I am in charge," she added, looking back at the rest of her class. Dwight chimed in that Dominque, not Chaucer, is in charge, and Kelli's young brigade agreed as a whole that Dominque was in charge.

Dwight then spoke up: "As the person in charge ..." As he began his answer, Ellie made a face in fun and Dwight smiled back. The older kids enjoyed the humor, but wished they could get back to the story at hand. Dwight continued, "We stick together and go onward. We will pray that if we are supposed to find the king, God will help us. That is what they do. I am sure of it."

Kalli turned the page and read a little bit to herself. She looked up at Dwight and turned her head to one side. "The young brigade thought about quitting, but instead they decided to pray for help and instruction," said Kalli, reading ahead. "How did you know that?" she asked Dwight.

Dwight smiled from ear to ear. He did not hesitate to let the other members of the brigade know, "If I were the leader, that is what I would do," but he felt a little guilty. "Have you not read this author before? He also writes old people's books. He's a Christian, and he always talks about God." Still feeling a little guilty, he continued, "Also my mom checked out this book from the library so that we can read it at night before I go to bed. You won't be able to wait to find out what happens in the next chapter."

A young soul after my own heart, Kalli thought, reading ahead. She had been exercising self-control, but now she was tempted. She was probably going to download the Kindle version, so she did not say anything about Dwight's bedtime story. "So that explains it, young Dominque. If you were in charge, would you pray for direction and enlightenment, even in such an impossible situation?" asked Kalli. She would not argue, since they clearly believed that God would help them find their way. After all, it was a child's book and they were children. "I will continue to read from where we left off, even though we already read ahead to find out what they will decide to do."

Leaning against the wall with her legs crossed and staring down at her phone, Sadie decided to add her take on the story. "Well, dear Dominque," she said sweetly, sitting down cross-legged next to Ellie, "it does tell us that 'Even the darkness is not dark to You; the night is bright as the day, for darkness is as light with You.' That is Psalm 139:12 in the English Standard Version. So that is a good choice, even if you already knew that was the choice they made. If anyone can see into the darkness, it is God, for it is as light to Thee." Dominque's thumb went up.

Margaret, one of the older children, raised her hand and said, "That was a good one, especially since I don't always go in dark places. I am not even allowed outside in the dark. But if I were in the dark, God would still watch over and guide me. If I ever find myself in a dark place,

God will be there." Margaret was not sure if what she had said made sense, but she knew she had a point.

What a bright ten-year-old, thought Kalli. She felt like she could apply the darkness to many aspects of her own life, but she did not want this to become a Bible study.

Another hand went up in the air. Sadie acted excited, and sadly Kalli wished she would go back to her phone. Sadie said, "Yes, Tina? Or should I call you Guinevere, the duchess, who longs to find her king?"

Tina blushed. She was glad that the young brigade with whom she sat on the floor did not include her king, for the implications would have been awful. Especially since she liked Arthur, the boy who sat next to her. Tina stood up and said, "Well, as Guinevere, I must say it is our duty to be light in the darkest places. The light that shines from within us is for all the world to see. Philippians 2:15 says, 'in the midst of a crooked and perverse nation, among whom ye shine as lights in the world.' That's the King James version." Then Tina made a curtsy and sat back down. As one of the oldest in the group, Tina had everyone laughing, especially the younger children.

Sadie giggled as well at the role-playing and the curtsy. Then she put her hands on her knees and asked, "Who is the light that shines within you?"

Role playing had been Kalli's idea, but not like this. This was out of control, but the whole group exclaimed at one time, "Jesus!" Sadie wanted to sing "This Little Light of Mine," but Kalli said, "No!" She was not going to let it turn into a Bible study. They had only a little time left, and Kalli wanted to get to the end of the chapter. She pretended not to be bothered by what had just happened, but she was extremely agitated. She felt like her brigade had been hijacked.

Kalli had an urge to go outside for a cigarette; she still smoked on occasion. She looked at the young faces once again and realized they were not her young faces but belonged to someone else. "Well, this has been loads of fun," said Kalli. "But let's get back to our story, shall we?" She began reading where she had left off.

★★★

Mom was grocery shopping for Kalli again. It was Mexican night, and she was preparing chicken enchiladas with green habanera sauce, refried beans, and a small cucumber salad with rice, tomatoes, and corn. She hoped Kalli was going to like all the ingredients, and she planned on making the meal as low fat as possible. She was using low-fat cheese and substituting cabbage for the tortillas. It was tricky, but she had tried it at home over the weekend and liked it.

She had been substituting ingredients for a few weeks now, and Kalli had recently started to notice and complain. Unfortunately all of Mom's good intentions had no lasting effects, for Kalli still had no problem finding high-calorie food. She ordered in quite a bit and even started ordering her own groceries when her mother stopped picking up some of the items on her list such as orange puffs, potato chips, and high-calorie ice cream. When her mother would remind her that pounds come on easily but come off much harder, Kalli shrugged with indifference.

The kale looked a little wilted today, but she was going to make it like collards anyway and boil it. She would ask for half price at the register; that would mean no self-checkout, but she was in no hurry. The cell phone buzzed in her coat pocket. She was sure it was Kalli wanting her to pick up some cream cheese for one of her dips.

She looked at her phone and saw that it was Coby. "Hey Coby! How are you?" she exclaimed. "Is everything all right?" She talked with Coby every day, but usually at night rather than during the day. She hoped it was not bad news. She expected Coby home for the holidays. He rarely was deployed for extended periods of time because of his certifications. He got to be more choosy about where he wanted to be. The checkout line was long, and she wished that she had not picked up the wilted kale.

"Yeah, everything is all right," said Coby. "I have good news and great news. I am going to Beirut, and they are moving me up the ranks. You can address me as Lieutenant Colonel Marshall in a few months, and I will be living there for a few years."

His mother held the kale up so the cashier could see it and laid it beside the conveyer belt. Then she took her groceries over to the self-checkout and swiped her rewards card. "Coby, did you really think that I would view you being stationed overseas for longer than a month as *good* news?" She could hear the sounds of keyboard typing.

Coby replied, "Mom, you and Kalli will be fine. This is my job and vocation. You're better off for having me here."

That was not her argument. Her argument was that she needed her only son with her. "I want to cry. I had made plans, travel plans, and Kalli is just starting to come around. Do you really want this to happen right now? Can't you wait one year before you move to Lebanon?" she exclaimed, trying not to sound anxious. She kept swiping groceries, but the barcode scanner was not reading them. She tried to pay attention, but she could not concentrate.

There was a long silence. "No, Mom, that is why I said it was both good news and great news. You know that it's good news, but you just don't think it's great news. But this is a huge break in my career, and it rarely happens like this. I would be a fool to let this opportunity pass me by, and they really need me here. I can't explain the details, since it is classified, but I need you to give me your full support. You and Kalli will be fine. I've prayed about this, and I know this is how it is to be for a little while. This will affect a lot of people in my life—not just you—and yet I know it's the right decision."

Coby's mother was silent, now paying for her groceries. "I don't know what to say, son. I think you're leaving us at the wrong time, but I will be happy for you if that's what you need." She wanted to be supportive, but it was hard. Their lives had been put on hold for Kalli's sake. Now Coby was taking his life off hold, but she was left literally holding the bag. She looked at her sack of groceries begrudgingly.

Coby knew it would be hard on his mother. They had grown closer over the past few years, especially since Kalli's accident. Coby had taken a leave of absence to take care of his family, and he had done his best not to regret that. But now it was time for him to go back to work and make a difference. This opportunity was a career changer.

He would not be in charge just of communications; he would be the officer in charge of the field base. If only his mother knew that he had met with General Cooper. He needed her to understand.

As she walked across the parking lot, she looked in her purse for the clicker fob to her car. When she found it, she pushed the unlock button, paying no attention to the gray Mercedes starting to back up. The car stopped inches from her, just as she dropped her groceries and hit the car with her right hand. The driver got out of the car to make sure she was okay.

She was physically fine, but emotionally a wreck. She exclaimed concurrently to her son and the Mercedes driver, who was helping her pick up her groceries, "Coby, I need you. I almost got hit by a car! That is how distracted I am ... Yes, I'm sure that I'm all right. No, I'm not going to sue you. No, I'm still standing. I'm right in front of you. I'm fine. My kumquats may sue you, but I'm still able to fix dinner for one of my children!"

The sweet Asian woman who had been driving the Mercedes was rather confused. "As long as you okay? I drive you home now. I call my husband. This not my first time," she admitted.

Coby's mom's eyes opened wide as she faced the woman who had nearly run her over. She would have blamed the driver, but she knew she should have seen the Mercedes backing out long before she walked behind it. "No, I will be fine. Thank you," she said. She took the groceries from the woman's hands and nodded her head slightly. The woman nodded back.

The single apple wedged between the tire and the

pavement would go untouched. Without warning, a peace encompassed Coby and Kalli's mother. The Asian woman smiled, such a genuine smile, and said, "God bless you." Then she got back into her Mercedes, though she waited for the parking lot to be clear of pedestrians before she drove away.

As Penny's, Coby's and Kalli's mother walked toward her car, she said nothing. Coby asked if she was okay, but still she said nothing. She had a profound, peaceful feeling that everything was going to be okay and Coby was going to do what he needed to do. "Coby, I am sorry. This is not your fault." She opened her trunk and placed her misshapen bag of groceries beside her spare tire. She needed to put it back in its proper place, but she had not found the time yet.

Her life would be harder, but she would be okay. Coby's life would be harder too, but the world would be safer—and he would be okay too. She was proud of both Coby and Kalli. She was even proud of Penny, although Penny had distanced herself from the family. Coby and Kalli both accepted change seamlessly, and Penny found it a little more difficult, but it was their mother who had a hard time coping.

The trunk slammed shut as Coby said, "Mom, it's going to be fine. Things work out the way they are supposed to work when we trust God. Nothing is perfect in the here and now. I don't know when it happened, but I have grown up. I'm thankful for my family, and I have been missing Dad a lot." Coby mentioned that he would be back soon and stay in the States for the next few months. He would leave after Valentine's Day. He would still have to work, since he would not be taking any more time off, but it would be normal hours. She was grateful to hear that they would have a few months together and be able to celebrate the holidays as a family.

Kalli waited at home for her mother to stop by with groceries and dinner. She had already prepaid for supper, which her mother would pick up. It was once again from her favorite Brazilian steak house. Her mother had stopped cooking anything with a lot of calories, and Kalli craved a large, fatty piece of red meat. She had considered adding fatty side dishes, along with the entree, but for the first time since her accident she actually wanted to lose weight.

Some of Kalli's close friends were coming over after work. She was excited but extremely nervous at the same time. She had seen most of them on various occasions, but not collectively as a group. When they used to hang out, it was "All for none, and none for all." She laughed at her own joke. They were self-absorbed, and nobody cared. The goal was to have fun, because work was far too serious. Sometimes they stepped on each other's toes, but somehow they all managed to stay friends over the years.

It would be a small party. She had arranged catering for twenty people, in case some of her friends brought friends. Most of the food would be vegan and vegetarian. Her best friends, Missy and Amy, were totally vegan, but they were always hungry, so she had picked out her own vegan favorites that were loaded with calories. They had ample grains, beans, and nuts, which she ate to keep from starving. Now she would binge on meat before they arrived and then eat like a bird while they were there.

The picture on the kitchen counter was the only one

that she had of all of them together. Everyone had been huddled together at Sid's house. She had been a couple of years younger then, but she looked pretty much the same now. She looked at her reflection in her phone and then at the photo—the same hairstyle and clothes, but she was not sure that she hadn't changed.

Her mom let herself in with only a slight knock at the door. The bag of groceries went down on the kitchen counter, followed by the take-out food from the restaurant and her phone. She placed her purse and coat on the bar stool. Without even greeting Kalli, she began unloading the bag of groceries into the fridge.

"Mom, are you okay?" asked Kalli. Previously she would have just waited patiently for her mother to tell her what was wrong, but she was different now. She had actually started to care.

The six-pack of beer went on the bottom shelf. "Yeah, I am. I did not see the beer you said to get except for the light version. That is a lie—the light version was on sale," said her mom, happy with her half-truth. Kalli shook her head as her mother continued to move things around in her refrigerator.

Kalli went into the kitchen, stopped within a few feet of her mother, and waited for her mother to give her all of her attention. "Mom, if the light version was on sale, the other stuff was probably on sale too. You just want me to drink light beer. I won't drink much of it. My friends who are coming over tonight usually bring their own drinks, but I still would have preferred something decent. They usually bring their own, but just in case."

The refrigerator started to beep as Kalli's mom

switched to unloading the non-refrigerated items. She opened the door, adjusted the seal, and shut the door tightly. Then she said, "I've got some bad news—excuse me, good news—from your brother."

Kalli wondered what news could be good for her brother but bad for her mother. She moved her chair closer to her mom, where she could hear every word her mom had to say. "He's engaged, isn't he?" she asked. "Who would have him? I'm just kidding. Is she nice?" She had a thousand more questions, but she would wait to make sure she had guessed correctly.

Her mother stopped what she was doing, looked at Kalli, and smiled. *What a beautiful daughter I have,* she thought. "No, he is going to Beirut in February for a couple of years, and he is going to be promoted to lieutenant colonel. It sounds like this will be an important move for him and a game changer, but I am just going to miss him—and I know you will too." Kalli took her mother's hands to console her.

The music was a little loud, but not enough to disturb Kalli's neighbors. Plus she had already let the association know, as part of their protocol, that she would be having guests and that there would be music, talking, and alcohol. Most people arrived around seven o'clock, which was a little earlier than Kalli had anticipated, but all the preparation was done. Before her mom had left, she had helped Kalli get everything ready for her friends.

Missy and Amy arrived first. They warmly hugged Kalli and gave her a framed picture of both of them in the office, along with a bottle each of red and white wine. They had wanted to arrive early to help with the preparations, but everything had already been done.

Sid arrived last. *That's just like Sid*, Kalli thought. *Always late to meetings, but always with the best presentations.* She would love to be back at the office in the thick of things with him, but what would she go back to? He had most of her residual clients, and Sid hated to share. *Oh Sid*, she thought, *I used to be so much better than you, but what have I become?*

Sid seemed to know what Kalli was thinking. He tilted his head and gave her his best George Clooney look as if to say, "You really think so?" Then he lifted his glass to her. He had a new friend with him, and they seemed to be getting along better than he did with most of the other acquaintances that he dated from time to time. "Hey, Kalli," he said, leaving his friend and walking over to where Kalli sat. "You are looking really good. How do you feel?"

Kalli set her sparkling water beside his drink on the small coffee table between them. "All things considered, I feel pretty good. Therapy is going well, and we are making progress. Although sometimes I feel as if I'm in the twilight zone of someone else's life, I'm making my way forward. How are you, Sid? Better question, how do you feel?" She teased him a bit, hoping he would feel like he was being put on the spot.

Sid gazed at her in wonder and then chuckled. His drink was low, but he did not need a refill just yet. "Oh Kalli, I feel a little left out. You asked everyone else to visit you in the hospital, but you told me not to come. I also wanted to swing by here on several occasions, but again you emphatically said no. I consider yours truly to be one of your bestest. Is there something you want to tell me?"

Kalli was rather embarrassed now, and not sure she had any reason for telling him not to visit. She could not think straight. Usually she had a witty comeback, but she was just drawing a blank. So she gave him a sincere but not very truthful answer. "It must have been the drugs, or I was self-conscious, worried that you might find me too hideous. After all, look at your new friend. She's … and she seems to get along with you." Kalli hoped the heat was off now.

The glass of Scotch he held was as empty as when he had first set it down. He rolled the ice around in it, but did not take a drink. "Um, what about last week? I wanted to see you. I called, but still no answer, no text, nothing. And Kalli"—he paused for a long moment—"Hideous? You hide it well."

Several feet away, John had been listening to their conversation. John could be bold and brazen, but he was quite sweet most of the time. "Seriously, Kal, you look more than amazing!" he exclaimed. "The plumpness in your face—well, not just your face—suits the new you. It makes you look a little fuller, and I think fuller women are in style now." John knew he was digging himself a hole that he probably would not be getting out of anytime soon, but he tried.

Without warning, the other conversations quieted. Sid's friend came and stood beside him, putting her hand with perfectly manicured nails on his shoulder and squeezing to let him know it was time to go. She seemed to Kalli to be the impetuous type.

Kalli could not think straight. She was a little dizzy, and John would not stop talking. He went on about how plus sizes were an untapped multibillion-dollar market. If Kalli could have slid off her chair and into the ground, never to be seen again, that would have been a better place for her than where she was now.

Kalli oddly started thinking about her mom and wishing she was still there, maybe because Kalli felt so out of touch with everyone. Amy and Missy walked over, not to save her from her awkward conversation, but to let her know that they were leaving to meet some friends at a pub downtown. There was no invitation to come with them, but rather a kiss on the check to let her know that they would call her tomorrow.

Sid had gotten up and walked outside to the patio with his girlfriend. Kalli finally regained her composure and whispered in John's ear in a hushed but firm tone, "Honestly, John, that was unnecessary. I can't even do damage control. Plus sizes, really? And what is your excuse for not coming to see me? Sid's excuse was valid," she added, throwing a glance out to the patio.

John looked down and admitted that he really did not have an excuse, but he said that he would try to come by again sometime.

Kalli told him not to bother. Thinking about who she used to be compared with who she was now, she wasn't sure she wanted to be reconciled.

Everyone left within the next hour. By ten o'clock, Kalli was alone. She would have been put off, but she realized that she had changed and this was the way her world would stay. She no longer had the money to spend on things that kept her in style, and she no longer needed to go to the places in vogue. She was even having more fun being mellow that she had living the fast life. She did not have to ask, *Could this be me?* She knew it was her—and that was okay.

Sid whispered something in his friend's ear as he held her arm. She smiled at him, looked briefly at Kalli, and then went to the bedroom to retrieve her gold-sequined purse. Before leaving, she thanked Kalli and told her it was a great party and studied her watch. She did not look back at Sid.

Sid sat down beside Kalli and said, "So you were saying, before we were so rudely interrupted. You can't stand me because ...?"

Kalli laughed and looked around at the empty room. Everyone except Sid was gone, but it had been a good night. Sid and Kalli talked about current events, old times, and their friendship. He left after midnight, but not before helping Kalli clean up.

Chapter 12

Beirut

The video screen came on and Coby's voice echoed throughout the room. Kalli said, "Hold on, Coby. I'll be there in a second. I am trying on a new blouse I bought today, and I think it's a little too tight. I think I am getting a little larger around the shoulders. Have you noticed? Not that you have been around, and the video screen adds ten pounds."

Following the sound of a door shutting, Kalli's round face appeared on Coby's twenty-five-inch screen. "Is that the new blouse?" he asked.

Kalli readjusted the screen on her kitchen counter and went backward so he could see her better. She did a little spin in her wheelchair. The image was blurry and then sharpened.

"That looks great, Kalli. It doesn't look too large at all. It looks like you have room to grow."

Kalli looked down at her arms. "Really, I have room to grow?" She looked down once more and pulled both arms forward to feel the fabric constrict. "I see what you did there, by the way. You said it didn't look too large." Then she smiled and said, "But you are right, it's not too snug. I have a little room yet. So any change since you talked with Mom two weeks ago? Are you still coming home this weekend?" Kalli had a thousand things to talk to Coby about, but she needed to ask her best questions first. He usually needed to leave within the first thirty minutes of their conversations.

Hungry little Pac-Men were running back and forth across the bottom of Coby's screen as he talked. "I am okay. Thank you for asking," he said. "Oh, that's right. You didn't ask, nor have you texted in a while. And yes, I will be home this weekend. Could you let Mom know that I have a friend picking me up at the airport, so she is off the hook?"

The video had changed angles, and Kalli now held her video device in her hands. Her face now took up most of his screen, since she had moved right in front of the camera. But he did not mind looking at his cute sister's chubby face, so he did not say anything.

The red ghost turned blue, and the race was on. Kalli's face got even larger. Not only could Coby see up her nose, but her pores now looked a bit like moon craters. Exhilarated, she asked, "How did you do that? What other effects do they have that you can change?" *Gads*, he thought, and turned off the animated extras. Kalli's face returned to a normal size and her video device was placed back on the counter.

Now the screen changed to little aliens chasing each other back and forth with little weapons and shouting random blurbs. Kalli let out a loud laugh, which made Coby laugh too. He turned down his speaker volume and said, "I was just wondering how it's going with the kids." As Kalli reached for her device again, Coby quickly turned the effects off, but it was too late. Big Kalli was back. She put her device on the cabinet once again. Coby was grateful—and careful not to do anything else until their conversation was over.

"It's great," Kalli said, "and I really look forward to it. They are so smart, and we are reading the best book, *Out of the Hidden Darkness*, by a well-known Christian author. Apparently he writes Christian children books as well as adult books. I have no interest in him as an author other than the book we're reading."

Coby was holding a copy of *Out of the Hidden Darkness* that a friend had sent him. "Yeah, it is interesting reading," he said, "but I would suggest reading some of his other books. Even out of all his children's books, this was not nearly as popular as any of his other books. I am glad to hear you're doing well and having a good time with my kids. I miss them and everyone else." Coby looked down at his notes and asked, "Do you work with the same people from the program every week?"

Kalli grimaced. "At first Bruce, Allen, and Sadie were switching off, but mostly it came to be just Sadie who's stuck with us. She really bothers me."

Coby took a pen and underlined Sadie's name on his notes. "Sadie's cool. It can't be that bad." He studied a miniature cuckoo clock that was behind Kalli. It was one of her most prized possessions. Coby and Penny had both desperately wanted to inherit it, but they had conceded their rights to Kalli, since she was the youngest.

The miniature German grandfather cuckoo clock was the only item from her father's study that Kalli had wanted. She had no idea what the clock meant to the family or even the story attached to the antique. Penny had made the argument that she was entitled to it as much as any other member of the family except their mother, who had been willing to part with a good many of their father's things. But Kalli had said it was the only item by which she would remember her father. As Coby remembered, it had been hard to resist her woeful pleas.

The clock struck ten o'clock, but no bird sprang out; it still kept time but no longer functioned as a cuckoo clock. Kalli continued to talk about Sadie. "At first, I could not get her to look up from her phone. She was always happily texting people, in a good mood, and giggling with the kids. She was the most annoying ever, but now it's far worse. For the last two weeks, she has been miserable. She keeps to herself unless the kids are talking about God, and then she still gets weird. By weird, I mean happy or enthusiastic—which is just weird."

Coby turned his attention back to his sister. "I don't know, Kalli. You can't be mad at someone for being upset. You just need to be a friend and wait it out."

Kalli picked up her video device and shook it. "Wake up. She needs to wake up and shake herself free. She acts like someone died, but if they did, that would be news to me." She looked at the clock and realized that the kids would be coming in an hour. "It would be okay if she was forlorn on her own time and by herself in her own little corner where she should live, in my opinion. But she is miserable around all of us, and she should be fired. Can you fire a volunteer for spreading bad mojo? Someone texts her, she reads the text, rolls her eyes, and puts her phone back into her pocket."

There was silence for a good three minutes. Kalli was being far too somber for her brother not to take her seriously. Kalli was reading her texts while Coby continued to write notes at his desk. He finally looked up and said, "It sounds like Sadie has been emotionally distraught for the last two weeks. You need to keep an eye on her and be a friend. I'll be home this weekend and try to straighten things out."

Kalli looked up like a deer caught in the headlights. "Oh no, Coby, that is not happening. I am not becoming friends with Sadie. She's not only a backward Christian, no offense, but also an emotional mess. I am glad to read to all these little disciples of Jesus, but to take on a grown adult who should know better and likes to pout for some unknown reason is too much for me."

Coby laughed, not because he thought she was funny, but because she was way off base. Then a Bible filled the screen and Coby said, "Kalli, it's real, and so is He. If you want to refute or make fun of what Christians believe, start with the basics. It's knowledge, not ignorance, so start with an understanding of who Jesus is. I would never survive out here without it." Kalli looked down, feeling a twinge of guilt.

"And cut Sadie some slack," added Coby. "She needs it."

Honestly, Kalli wondered, *why did he pick me to read to these children?* She definitely needed them more than they needed her. In candor, she looked to those little ones to provide answers. They seemed to know so much, and she seemed to know nothing at times. She had no idea how they knew to pray and to surrender their lack of knowledge to God, but somehow there was a truth that persevered through their knowledge. Truth was always there for them, but could that be everyone's truth—one absolute? How did that make any sense? Kalli tried not to be frustrated and realized she had less than a half hour to get ready and eat before the children arrived.

"Coby, I will try to do better. I can hardly wait until this weekend to see you in the flesh." Then Kalli's phone buzzed, and she saw a text titled "How to Change Effects on Video Chat." She thanked Coby and hung up the phone.

The sea-green uniform that hung behind him was pressed and ready to go. Coby would once again slip into it and make his way down to the comms unit. With digital information now the heartbeat of the unit and infrastructure, central to military intelligence, it was essential that he train the next person on command to be as diligent and observant as he was—or even better. It helped that he never manned his position tired or expecting to be bored. He was never hung over, intoxicated, or under the influence, all of which would take away from the mission and position itself. It could also warrant disciplinary action.

The communication expert also needed to stay current, culturally relevant, and work well with the other departments. The more details that could be obtained from the surrounding areas and other intra-departmental sources, the better. It was then important to know how to disseminate it.

Coby found himself always in the know, even down to the minutest detail with regard to the culture and cultural influences, and it never worked against him. Even if he was not fluent in the language, he spoke enough of it to understand what was going on in any situation. His performance was based on passing on essential data to the team, so discernment was key. Although some of the operational logistics may have been above his clearance level, as on occasion he was told by a general onsite, he still needed to be able to decipher information and pass it on through the proper channels.

Coby loved his job, and he was not sure that the job to which he was being promoted would be as satisfying as his current role. But in the military, at times it was more about being flexible and going with the flow. Playing his part in the big picture was more important than just looking out for his own interests. Being in command of many folks, rather than just a few, could feed his insecurities, but no matter what lay in front of him, Coby would put his best foot forward.

Working the screens beside Sergeant First Class Collins was a young man with blond hair, horn-rimmed glasses, and a wiry smile. Coby stood behind them watching. The young man started to stand up to salute, but Coby put his hand on his shoulder and told him to be at ease. The communications specialist was exempt from certain formalities if it interrupted his command.

First Sergeant Collins tensed up. She looked up at Coby, nodded, and made her formal greeting. "So what are we looking at right here?" Coby asked, pointing at the screen. Sergeant Collins, one of the best, said they were watching a small gathering of the Progressive Socialist Party. Coby was surprised. As a specific area of the screen was enlarged, the dots grew into a tall, well-defined group of people. Specific leaders could be identified, though they weren't named as part of protocol, but Coby recognized most of them. They were nonthreatening, but sometimes they were linked with something else that was going on.

The first sergeant looked at the recruit and back at her screen. "The group had communist ties during the civil war, and it was associated with the People's Liberation Army. They adhere to the Druze faith, which believes in one god. Their highest population is here," she said, pointing on another screen to the rural mountainous areas east and south of Beirut.

Mildly impressed, Coby nodded and said, "It's one of the Lebanese Muslim communities along with Sunni; Shia; Alawi, a member of the Shiite group; and Ismaili, also part Shiite. Can you show me the Druze Chouf region of Mount Lebanon?" he asked. Collins did so on another screen, and they zoomed in on various geographical areas. "If something was brewing with the Hezbollah, as in the past, it would be evident. I'll take over now," Coby said to First Sergeant Collins. He introduced himself to his replacement. He would be working alongside Collins and the new recruit.

★★★

The kids filed in the door by twos. Sadie was last. She barely looked up at Kalli and waved slightly with her right hand. "Hi, Kalli," said Sadie. "Ready for another chapter of *Out of the Hidden Darkness*? Ooh, this looks great," she added, noting the spread of healthful food set out for the children on the table and countertop.

The children helped themselves to the variety of garden vegetables and hummus. They tried not to take too much, but there was plenty. Although lunch would be served in an hour and twenty minutes, Sadie was not concerned that they would fill up on vegetables. Kalli had asked if it was all right for the kids to have a nutritious snack before lunch, though she had not said it would be so plentiful. Everyone always looked forward to lunch, which sometimes made story time go too slowly for the children. Kalli thought that with a snack, the kids would not be so hungry during her readings.

Kalli was not even concerned that they would ruin her carpet or furniture. She told the kids to each make a one-time plate of food and bring it into the living area. It was all about reading time for Kalli.

Sadie studied Kalli, but soon lost interest. Sitting on the big easy chair, custom built to match the rest of Kalli's decor, Sadie made herself comfortable. She even used the throw behind her to surround herself in warmth.

Looking at Sadie, Kalli tried to like her, but her only thought was that she now would need to wash her favorite afghan. Then it occurred to her that quaint little blankets and pillows would make great gifts for the children. She could sew little throws and pillows for everyone. Even though she had never sewed a stitch in her life, she knew it was not beyond her capabilities. Her mother knew how to sew. In fact, it seemed that every woman from her mother's generation knew how to sew and cook. Kalli could ask her to help, which would be exciting for her mother since she lived and breathed for her. Kalli could make *everyone* happy.

The book chapter started out in a city by the ocean. The small brigade made its way out of the darkness of the deep forest and found themselves on a path that led a tiny merchant town by the water. When they emerged from the forest, the sun was so bright that they had to shield their eyes with their hands. The merchant town did not use its ports for exporting or importing. Instead the people sold fish and common goods since most of them, from what the brigade members could tell, were fishermen. The group was not properly greeted as people associated with royalty. In fact, they were ignored as though they were mere commoners.

They wondered if the town was under the king's domain, since they saw no flags flying. They compared their own clothes to those of the townspeople and noticed that the fabric and stitching were different. The clothes of the townspeople were not in layers, but simply stitched and less decent. In fact, most of the townspeople would have been taken into custody under the king's authority. They held tiny little devices that seemed to tell them what to do. "This is an odd place indeed, but we must continue on task," said Dominque.

The group stood in a huddle as they watched townspeople walk by, never looking up but only down. They would use their fingers to tap, and then tap again and again until they did something different. The king's company looked at each other in bewilderment. No longer were they on a dark path that would lead them to a hidden darkness and inevitably to the king, but rather in a town that was as bright as day and apparently not under the king's rule.

Kalli surveyed the children's faces that surrounded her. They were hooked on the story even more than on the snacks piled on the plates in front of them. She continued to read: "Guinevere grabbed Giovanni's arm. She had never been scared before entering the town, even when wild animals surrounded them, but now she was terrified. It seemed to her that the townspeople were all dead in some way. They were sleeping, yet awake, as if the queen had gotten to the town before them. They were just like the king." Kalli now started to distrust the story line and wished she had read ahead as to explain better the story to the children.

Alli raised her hand, and others' hands shot up as well. "Ms. Kalli, are they in New York?" asked Alli. When Kalli shook her head, Alli said, "But they all have cell phones, right?"

Kalli smiled. This was going to be a tough read. She assigned the children their characters, as they continued to ask questions and decide the fate of the small company in this strange town.

The doorbell rang before they had even finished their first chapter. They had discussed everything from modern technology to where the group should go now that they were out of the darkness, but they still needed to find the king. Sadie looked neither pleased or unpleased. *That's because no one has said the name of Jesus yet*, thought Kalli.

Lunch was bland compared with the hummus and vegetables. But snack food was usually rated higher than lunch—unless lunch included pizza. In this case it was peanut butter and jelly sandwiches, potato chips, and a cookie. Kalli wanted to swap the potato chips and cookies for something more healthful, but the kids had already eaten most of their lunch before she thought to do so. The person on lunch duty that day must not have put much thought into it, but Kalli knew the children would be grateful for anything. They definitely appreciated her snacks, and although she would not boast, she did pat herself on the back.

Kalli's refrigerator was now stocked with low-calorie, healthful, mostly vegan choices. She had been doing better in therapy as her workouts had started to intensify, which led to higher-quality eating habits and a better diet plan, at the prompting of her family. She had been trying to lose a little weight, although her mom had teased her about it, claiming that it was because of Kalli's new friend with whom she now talked almost every night. But Kalli insisted that Sid wasn't a new friend—he had *always* been a friend—and bad eating had just been a phase that helped her get through her sadness. Her mother could definitely see that, and she was glad that Kalli had realized it sooner than later.

The children voted to continue the story instead of hanging out for the time they had left. Kalli's reading pace had slowed as she had become more animated, so Sadie asked if she could step in and read some, just for the sake of time. Trying to read only the highlights, in order to speed things up, Sadie began:

In this city of light, there was a small fish shop with a cross on the door, the only sign that the king's company recognized, so they decided to go inside. They asked within the shop about any hidden places that the queen would go.

"This is it, and you should leave the way you came," cried the owner of the shop. "This is the hidden darkness in which you traverse. All of this city is the queen's. It is hidden in the darkness and beaming with natural light, but it lacks what brought you in here, the cross."

His wife had approached his side, but she would not look at the children.

"Yes, but we come in the name of the king," said the young brigade.

Sadie finished the chapter, which was a relief since she and Kalli wanted to finish up in a timely manner as part of protocol. Etiquette was becoming more formalized as the children's program increased in popularity. Kalli was on board with all the regimentations, since she associated certain protocols with the safety of the children. She was not sure if she still liked the story, and she wondered if there was a protocol about the reading content.

The doorbell rang again, and Casidy, the driver, appeared in the doorway. He was eager to collect the kids and be on their way. Some of the little girls hugged Kalli as they were leaving. "Thank you, Miss Kalli, for your reading," said Alli. Others added their thanks for the snacks, and someone told her to keep them coming—which she had every intention of doing.

Chapter 13

Family, Friends, and Foes

Kalli decided to venture out and do her own shopping. She had been to the store a handful of times, but mostly she had let her mother do her shopping and cooking. Kalli knew that eventually she would have to improve and become more independent, but for now she was okay with their routine. Still finding her way, she was in no hurry.

The Fresh Market was an organic-rich, high-end place to shop. It had its own cafe, which was vegan and organically based, although the market itself did sell fish, meat, and poultry. It also had a coffee shop, written up in a local newspaper as a great place for singles to meet. Kalli could not see it, but she wasn't interested anyway.

Fred Catchum pulled up to the front door. Kalli was glad that he no longer insisted on pulling into the space for people with disabilities and taking her to the door. Even if he had insisted, she would have refused. "Are you sure, Kalli? I would love to do your shopping with you. I need a few things as well," he said, helping her out of the car and into her chair.

Kalli sweetly smiled up at him and firmly grabbed his hand, which was resting on her right shoulder.

Fred couldn't decide whether to wait for her in the parking lot or just quit. This was not the only way he earned his income. Fred mostly like Kalli and treated her differently from most of his clients. She was a no-nonsense, down-to-earth type of gal. But this time he saw something different in her smile, which he realized was a disguise for contempt—or something even worse. Kalli believed that she was better than him.

The wheelchair was secure and in the locked position. "No, Fred, and please go back to calling me Ms. Marshall. Park the car in the parking lot and wait for me until I let you know differently." Then she added, "But I appreciate your attempt to treat me special." With her wheelchair no longer locked, Kalli took control.

Fred watched as someone held the door open for her and she began her shopping experience. He was professional on most levels, but he really wanted to give her the finger for all to see. Instead, he muttered it under his breath. He turned around and returned to his gray 2019 GLA 250 SUV Mercedes-Benz and refrained from its tires. The automobile had been converted to serve passengers with disabilities, for which he could charge a higher rate. If he ever changed occupations, he could always change it back and trade it in.

Kalli didn't even notice the bump as she rolled over a bag of flour that had been dropped on the floor and was now partly stuck to her tires. Her mind was no longer on

Fred, but accessibility in general. She would talk to the accountant who managed her investment fund from the accident. She hoped to make obtaining an automated car a priority in the near future. After all, the stock market was up and she could get a vehicle for less than twenty thousand dollars.

The electric Chairiot solo car was at the top of her wish list. Chairiot Mobility had produced an electric car designed for people with disabilities. The back of the car opened up for wheelchair access, and then she'd be on her own for driving, with some technology assistance.

Kalli stopped in the produce aisle. The tomatoes looked extra red—if only she liked tomatoes, but she had tired of them as an adolescent. Then she saw organic kale, which was tricky because it tasted horrible unless she cooked it. Also any organic produce needed to be washed at least twice. Kale was hard to wash, but she still preferred it even if it was a pain.

Kalli's mind was still on kale when she spotted Sid's friend, whose name she could not remember. The woman—whom Kalli just thought of as Nameless—stood there polishing an apple with her sleeve and preparing to take a bite. Nameless glanced around, and she and Kallie locked eyes. Kalli would have avoided being spotted at all costs, but it was too late, and there was nowhere to hide. Nameless was surprised to be caught, but what did it matter? Taking a large bite of the apple, she walked over to greet Kalli.

Kalli thought, *What are the odds? Hardly any people go to the grocery store at this time of day!* Prepared for the worst, she said, "Hey, I think you were at my party a few weeks ago." Maybe Nameless would introduce herself.

Some of the apple fell from her mouth as Nameless replied, "Yes, I remember. A party—not happy hour? Sid spoke very highly of you at that party. Well, it was nice not meeting you." She remembered that they had not been introduced at the party, and she guessed that Sid had mentioned her name to Kalli, who had later forgotten it. Nameless headed toward the next aisle.

Pretending to examine the kale, Kalli kept her eye on Nameless. She had said that Sid spoke well of Kalli, which could mean that Nameless and Sid were no longer dating. Also, Kalli talked with Sid almost every night, and while Kalli seldom asked about anyone, Sid often threw out names. Surely he would have mentioned Nameless at least once or twice if they were still dating. Kalli and Sid tended to talk about matter-of-fact subjects. She tried not to let things get too personal with him, but they talked about almost everything else.

"What's your name?" asked Kalli.

The apple was already three-fourths eaten. With the back of her hand, Nameless wiped juice from her chin like it was not a thing. She walked back to the produce aisle, stopped within a few feet of Kalli, and said, "My name is Alexa, Kalli."

Kalli thought, *There's no way I would forget that name. Every time I asked the lights to turn on or requested weather information, I would think of Sid's almost girlfriend.*

Alexa continued, "Sid and I were close, very close. We saw each other off and on for three months. He said that I was one of the few people with whom he was ever serious."

The apples now looked enticing. Kalli filled a clear bag with five of them. She wasn't sure what Alexa wanted from her, but she wasn't going to feel sorry for her. Kalli had known Sid too long, and that was just his way. He was always processing but never committing, and nobody would ever change that.

Kalli said sarcastically, "Alexa, that is a name not to forget; it's special." Then she pulled out one of the apples and handed it to Alexa, who looked surprised as she held it. Kalli took a moment. "Oh, that's right," Kalli said. "You had your, um, apple" She grabbed the apple back and stuck it in her bag and added, "I guess I'll keep it." Alexa turned her back to Kalli and walked away.

Kalli shopped for a few more items before checking out. In line at the register, she texted, "Sorry. Please pick me up at front." Fred immediately texted back, "I'm just checking out now. Look to your right." They turned and waved at each other.

★★★

Saturday finally happened. Kalli had wanted to be at the airport when her brother arrived, but he told her not to come. Someone else would be picking him up at the airport, and he'd be fine. He would see them that evening.

Sadie waved, trying to look casual as Coby walked toward baggage claim. She looked at her phone and waved again. He picked her up, hugged her and set her back down. Taking his face between her hands, Sadie looked him square in the eyes and said, "I love you, Coby Marshall. That's why this is so darn hard. There is nothing you can say that will make this okay. Let's just go. If you want to talk about it, we can do that in the car. By the way, your sister hates me."

Coby just chuckled as they continued toward baggage claim. Sadie let him hold her hand firmly, but she did not do the same to his. He had to make things right, and she could not even entertain the notion of a long-distance relationship. She needed more consideration from him than that, something that said he would not be leaving her for long.

Sadie had not gotten a full night's rest in over two weeks. She had puffy eyes from crying in the car on her way to pick him up. Coby could tell she had been crying, because her mascara had run. Not much, but enough to notice. Still, he thought she was beautiful—tall with straight blond hair, freckles, and blue eyes that sparkled when she laughed. Sadie was one of the few women he had ever known who were better looking without makeup. He noticed that she had lost weight while he was gone, and he wished she did not take his absence so hard. He had promised her that they would figure things out when he got home, but she had already figured things out for both of them.

★★★

Kalli sat on the couch and picked up her notebook, half full of story ideas, from the coffee table. None of the ideas she had written down seemed to mean anything to her. She wanted to write a story that didn't short sell the criminal justice system, but she did not know enough about criminals or justice to sink her teeth into anything. She did not even like detective stories or suspense thrillers, so she asked herself why she wanted to write about something that didn't pertain to her at all.

The pages turned. There must be some story line that she could evolve into a novel. Perhaps one about a girl who goes missing as a result of bad blood between an agent and a former agent who turned rogue? But what did she know about being an agent? Maybe a dull novel about someone who needed to cope with some harsh circumstance in their life. Someone who just needed hope, but had a hard time finding it with friends and family. Someone who needed to start over. She could relate to that, but she really wanted to write about unsolved mysteries in the criminal justice system.

Starting at page one, Kalli again turned the pages of her black composition notebook. There must have been close to three hundred entries, but there it was at the bottom of the third page. She had written it in blue ink, not black, so it stood out from the rest of the page. Only three sentences, but that was enough: "Hit-and-run accident, the driver who got away. There were no tags and no reason. The second driver who was also at fault had to pay, but what was the price for her life?"

Too familiar, it gave Kalli chills. She wondered if subconsciously she had overlooked it for a reason. She needed to write the story of her accident—no justice, the driver who had sped away—but rather than being about her, she would write it as fiction. Anything else would be too draining, and she really needed to keep moving forward in her thoughts and actions. If she had anything to work through, she would do that with a counselor.

Kalli had no luck getting on the schedule of her old counselor, but the "dear doctor" always seemed to be accessible. She would get on a regular schedule with him within the week. She had promised both her mom and Coby that she would find someone in whom she could confide about her life.

The video screen announced a call from Sid, but Kalli was not sure she wanted to talk with him right then. First, she finally thought she could write a few hundred words, so she did not want to lose her momentum. Second, she did not look her best. She had just finished therapy and was hungry and sweaty. Still, she figured it did not have to be a long conversation. "Hi, Sid," she said. "To what do I owe the pleasure?"

The video screen froze with Sid's face in transition, his eyes half shut. It was weird, looking at him like that, waiting for him to come back to life, but that was the future, she thought. She figured the screen would unfreeze in a few seconds, as long as their slow internet connection didn't cut off completely, and she was right. She soon heard Sid's voice ask, "So is it okay if I stop by?"

Looked around the apartment, Kalli replied, "I missed some of that. You want to stop by? Why?"

Sid laughed. "I was saying that I'm in the area and I picked up some ice cream for us. You said you liked Dutch apple meringue, the flavor of the month at your favorite ice cream shop, NM's Dairy. Since we're nearing the end of the month, I thought I'd try it."

Kalli studied his face, easing herself off the couch and

getting closer to the video screen. "Yeah, is that right?" She had stopped paying attention to his words and was studying the screen, noticing where he was walking.

Sid continued, "So I did, and you have incredible taste in ice cream. Who knew apple and meringue added to ice cream would taste delicious?"

Kalli recognized the well-manicured lawn, parked cars, and entryway to a building. As Sid continued to talk, she noticed an elevator to his right, which meant he had parked in the outside lot, not the garage. When she saw the gray walls and familiar painting, she shouted, "Are you outside my door?" at the video screen. She went to unlock her door, opened it wide, and asked, "What if I had said for you not to come because I plan on being busy?" Her question was serious, but she held open the door. The ice cream was melting and running down the sides of the cups. She stayed in the doorway for a moment before letting him squeeze by and step over the threshold.

"I would turn around and take my ice cream with me," said Sid. "It would be as if I had never asked the question."

Kalli realized that she was being a bit negative, especially since most people didn't mind friends dropping in from time to time. She should have moved her chair, but it wouldn't budge. "Oh," she said, holding out her hand for the ice cream, which Sid handed to her. He wanted to take the liberty of moving her wheelchair into the kitchen with him, but he knew she'd object. *Someday*, he told himself.

Kalli gingerly rolled herself into the kitchen. It was a bit awkward since the ice cream was melting and messy, but she had placed napkins on her lap beneath the cup of ice cream. She pushed her chair next to Sid's and said, "This really is good. It's decadent, like baked Alaska combined with my mother's deep-dish apple pie." Sid continued to eat without looking up at her.

Ice cream was one of the items that Kalli was supposed to stay away from until she was back to her normal weight. But it made her so happy that she thought about forgoing her better eating habits altogether. She just wanted to be okay, and ice cream made everything seem normal again. "I like it," she said. Having finished her own, she watched Sid eat his. Longing for just one more scoop, she spotted the bag sitting next to him. Could it be? It looked like it had room for at least a pint.

Sid said, "I almost forgot. Can I put this in your freezer?" He had noticed Kalli staring at the bag. Having decided not to indulge in a second scoop, Kalli didn't say anything. Sid walked over and opened the freezer. "I got us two pints of the Dutch apple meringue, one for you and one for me," he said, moving things in the freezer to make room.

The thought of Sid as a boyfriend popped into Kalli's head—but was immediately rejected. Sid was Sid, and she really couldn't handle anything more than that from him. Maybe after she figured out the whole life thing. When he sat back down with her, Kalli said, "I went through my story ideas and came across one that I'll be able to write. It's about a man who gets into a near-fatal car accident. He's on a quest to find out whether it was an accident or he was a target of some plot." Actually it didn't sound very well thought out, and she wondered if it would play out well.

Looking directly into her eyes, Sid said, "Well, it sounds like something that has probably been done before. But as long as you write well and make it your own, it should be incredible. I have never known you to do anything less than excellent." In general he avoided giving compliments, but this was the truth, though Kalli wondered why he had said it. "Speaking of excellent," Sid continued, "I was hoping we could go over some client info together."

Kalli's ice cream cup was empty. She came close to helping herself to seconds, even though she had decided against it. If Sid could only read her mind, he would suggest a cup for himself and then ask if she would like seconds too. Kalli waited, but no such suggestion was made. It was such a struggle that she now hoped Sid would leave—and soon, so she could get back to writing her novel and eating ice cream.

"Sure. So you really think so?" she asked. "It could be excellent? I don't know a lot about criminal justice novels. I don't even like detective stories, movies, or television shows."

Sid put the plastic spoons and abandoned plastic cups in the trash. He wished he had asked for two scoops, but the Kalli he used to know would have been insulted if he had assumed that she would eat more than one scoop. He preferred only a small portion of anything with sugar but sometimes he made an exception.

The black composition book was on the couch where

Kalli had left it. As a habit, she did not ask anyone except her mother to get anything for her.

Sid was not going back to the table, because he'd rather sit somewhere more conducive to a quiet conversation. He said, "Yes, really. Just look what you've done with your condo. I remember when you were renovating and would bring swatches to the office to get our opinions. Everything you suggested was hard to imagine, but this place is top notch. Anything that you put your heart and soul into will turn out great." Sid was a fan.

The living room wall was layered shiplap painted a grayish blue. Sid had never seen it done that way, but again, he was a fan. The back wall reminded him of a cloudy day, and he was thinking he could do something similar to one of his walls. The recessed lighting, which Kalli controlled with her phone or video device, gave the room a soothing feel. She had adapted several of her fixtures for smart devices.

Sid had brought some information that he wanted Kalli to look over with him. It was in his jacket, which he had not yet bothered to take off. He pulled out a folder containing a list of office client information, along with some tickets to a show and another envelope. While he sat on the couch and waited for Kalli to join him, he looked at her notebook.

"I guess we're here now," Kalli said as she moved into the living area. Only a few feet away, it was cozier than the kitchen. "I really appreciate the compliment. I do remember going over all of the details with you, but you weren't much help."

Sid said that he thought he had been helpful, as she

had asked about every single detail whether it made sense to him or not.

The blue folder, already bent in half, wasn't very thick, so Sid just slid it between the seat cushions for the time being. "Do you mind?" he asked, picking up Kalli's notebook and thumbing through her ideas.

Kalli felt vulnerable again, but she wasn't quick enough to snatch it out of his hands. Her large couch had plenty of room, but Sid sat in the center, which made it hard for Kalli to maneuver without being unwieldly. She went to one side of the couch and pulled Sid's folder from between the cushions. "Do *you* mind?" she asked, looking at the contents. "These are my clients, not your clients. What do you want, more information so that if I ever return and try to steal them back, I won't be able to because you've coddled them?"

A pair of airline tickets to LaGuardia fell out of the folder and landed on the floor. Sid snatched them up as Kalli started to move to the couch. He instinctively grabbed her by the waist and lifted just enough so that she was next to him on the couch. He knew if it had not appeared effortless, she wouldn't have said anything, but it would have been ackward. He said, "So I guess I'll start with the tickets and work my way backward, since you already guessed at the other stuff."

Kalli was right. Sid was there to cement all her clients and years of hard work for himself. *So why am I not more angry?* she asked herself. *Oh, that's right. I no longer work there or plan on going back to work right now. Still, starting from scratch would suck.*

Her black notebook was now at the far end of the

couch, where Sid had tossed it when the tickets fell from the folder. "By the way," he said, "you should keep writing. Some of your ideas are pretty interesting."

He was really getting on Kalli's nerves. In fact, she thought that she should have been *more* angry at him. But somehow, despite the appearance of a hostile takeover, she knew everything was okay. She wanted to work herself up into a bother, but trust was the only emotion she really felt. Was something wrong with her brain that the doctors had overlooked? No, when she had been touch-and-go in the hospital for a while and they hadn't known what to expect, they'd done all sorts of tests, including a CT scan.

Sid wondered what Kalli was thinking, but she said nothing. As he explained himself, she held on to the client list. "So go on: what is it you want to know about your clients?" asked Kalli.

He grabbed her hand, the one holding the list. The airline tickets were a stretch, but he hoped everything would go as planned. "I respect your hard work," said Sid. "Believe me, Kalli, your clients do not want to work with me, and they keep asking when you're coming back. Talk about finesse ... The questions are beside the clients' names." He watched her study the piece of paper like she was searching for the right answer on a multiple choice test.

Finally Kalli asked, "Okay, what gives? All the information you need to know is quantitative, data driven, and already in the clients' portfolios. You know this."

Sid shook his head and pointed to a handwritten question beside a client's name. "*That's* it. I need to quantify their needs in relation to our new products.

If I hit some of our current clients first, we'll have our own little beta group, even though our products, which come from acquisitions, are not really beta. Instead of drumming up new business for these products, I could sell to some of our known clients first—*if* there's a need. What do you think?"

Looking at the names, Kalli got very excited. Never good with boundaries, she twisted even closer to Sid and leaned into him. Since she was familiar with their products, it was not hard for her to extrapolate. She held out her hand, and Sid handed her his pen. "This client has a human resource need and a recruiting department of about twenty," said Kalli, invigorated. When she looked up at him and smiled, he smiled back.

The airline tickets temporarily went back into Sid's pocket. He was glad that Kalli was already familiar with the new products. "So are you thinking about coming back to work?" he asked. "I was told that you're on a sabbatical of sorts and that if you do come back, it won't be until next year."

Kalli said nothing, but continued to write notes on the client list—the best contact, to the best of her memory, for the department along with additional information. When she finished and handed the list back to Sid, she said, "Yeah, I do miss it. I'm familiar with the acquisitions and the new services and products that we offer. I think sometimes we spread ourselves too thin as a company, but best of luck. What I wrote down should help." She was still attached to working at her old company, but she was okay with letting go for now. "I'm not sure if I'll go back, but if I do, I'll steal my clients back from you," she said somberly.

Here comes the stretch, Sid told himself. "Hey, I have two tickets to New York to see a play, in case you're interested ... to thank you for helping me out. The play isn't well known, but it should be. It's not Broadway, but it's quaint."

Kalli had moved farther from him, and now she wished that she was sitting in the kitchen. She started to feel uncomfortable and did not have any place to go. "It sounds like fun, but I'm not interested in dating." It was the only answer she could muster.

Sid knew to take it slow with Kalli. "I'm sure you're familiar with the story, but this play stars an incredibly talented actor when he's in town, and I have it from a good source that he *will* be performing. Do you remember how you said we should go to New York, shop, and see a play?" He knew he didn't have to remind her, and that he was coming off as desperate. If only he had not asked that last question, but he had one more thought that could make it seem more casual. From his pocket, Sid pulled the airline tickets and six tickets to the play.

Kalli was relieved to see the additional tickets. "I believe I said that to a group of us, but I guess you took it to heart, so thanks," she said. "So this would *not* be a date? Who else did you invite? Is anyone from the office coming?" She was thinking this could be an opportunity to get back in with some of her friends.

Sid admired her brashness, though he secretly hoped no one else would accept the invitation. He took back the tickets, shoved them back into his pocket, and said, "Yeah,

I offered them to anyone, but they have to come up with their own airline tickets and hotel rooms. I blocked off a few rooms, including two rooms for us, across the hall from each other for two nights. Sound good?"

Kalli wasn't sure how smoothly everything would go. She wasn't as mobile as she used to be, but she didn't want to stop living her life. Sid was also the perfect travel partner, which made it easy to say yes. When they had traveled together for business, it had always been productive and exciting. He was funny and always positive, to the point that it was irritating, but somehow things did seem to work out for him. After all, he now had most of her residual client base, which was a real reason to be positive.

Despite that one annoying and unrealistic attribute, his other attributes put him at the top of his game. Sid was the most resourceful, professional, fun coworker she'd ever had. But this trip to New York would be for fun, rather than work. "Are you sure you wouldn't rather take Siri?" Kalli asked, not realizing she had made a mistake.

Sid laughed and said, "Do you mean Alexa?" He picked up her notebook and set it on the coffee table for her.

Kalli wondered what had gone wrong in Sid and Alexa's relationship. "Yes, I'm sorry. I told myself I would never forget that name, but it's so close to Siri. I ran into her at the grocery store, and she still likes you. I mean, she *really* likes you, as in wanting a future together, and she said that you feel the same."

Surprised, Sid stood up as if he was going to leave. "She's not the one," he said, "but for a short time I wasn't sure what to think. We were getting to know each other, but I knew that it was not forever. Not that anyone is looking for forever these days," he added with a shrug.

Kalli sat quietly, wanting to know more, but Sid did not want to say anything else. He knew that she spooked easily and that she wasn't a forever type of gal. Finally Kalli asked, "What else?"

The clock chimed. Sid had noticed at the party that the bird no longer came out. It wouldn't be an easy fix, but he knew a guy. "I really don't like to talk about my relationships with other people," he said, "but yes, Alexa is one of the better people I've dated." Bending down to give Kalli a hug, he said, "Well, I've taken enough of your time. I'll call you tonight, after you have dinner with your brother and mom. Also, New York is a couple of months from now. Tell your mother and brother I said hello."

Chapter 14

The Throwback

Kalli's condo was the new family hangout. It was just easier for everyone to come there since it was centrally located, and Kalli preferred it most of the time. Mom was early and had started to prepare all of Coby's favorites. She had picked up a prime rib from a local market that sold special cuts of meat. She used a garlic marinade and put actual cloves of garlic within the outer rim of the roast, which smelled heavenly. She had also mashed potatoes and roasted vegetables, and two days earlier she had made dough for sourdough rolls—Coby's absolute favorite.

Kalli was wearing the shirt that she had showed Coby when she talked with him last. She still felt like it was a little tight, but she'd be losing weight soon as she continued to eat better and exercise more. The ice cream earlier that day had been a lapse of judgment, she told herself. Sid, too, might be a lapse of judgment, as she thought about New York and how impossible that trip would be. It would take her hours to do anything, compared with what traveling had been like before the accident.

She'd talk with her mother and brother privately

and ask them their advice. She wasn't sure about New York, but the old Kalli wouldn't have been unsure about anything. She just didn't fit in with most of her friends from her old job anymore, and Sid was trying too hard to make everything right for her. She assumed that's why he had set the trip up.

Coby called from his car. "I'm on my way and should be there shortly. Mom, is that prime rib that I smell, along with my favorite rolls?" He laughed, knowing his mother would fix only his favorites, since she had asked him about that several days ago.

Looking at the video device, Coby's mom wondered if it transmitted smells too, but she knew better than to ask. The rolls were just coming out of the oven and would still be warm when he got there. The smell of bread filled the air. "Yes, I asked what you wanted, and you said the usual—all of your favorites," said his mother. "I was hoping you could pick up some of that ice cream that Kalli likes." Coby agreed and ended the call.

In the bedroom, Kalli was not sure exactly what her mother had said. But she didn't volunteer the fact that she had two pints of her favorite ice cream in the freezer until she was out of the bedroom. "There should be two pints of ice cream already in the freezer, Mom."

Her mother checked the freezer. "Coby is probably already in the parking lot at NM's. He was in the area when he called. Are you sure there are two pints? I see only one."

Kalli went into the kitchen and looked for herself. "He took it. I was hoping he'd forget." She tried to remember when Sid could have taken his pint. Probably toward the end of the afternoon, before he left but after he said goodbye. Preoccupied with her writing, she had not seen him to the door.

The doorbell rang, and Coby let himself in. He had a present for Kalli, a typewriter. She had told him that she wanted one so that she could concentrate on her writing and not be distracted. She hoped it would make writing easier for her. A typewriter was better for her eyes and more ergonomically sound, depending on where she put it. Then she could scan and edit the story when she finished writing. Computerized typewriters could do the editing as well, but word processing software was the better choice.

Setting the ice cream on the table, Coby said, "It's a throwback, and it was expensive, but I agree that it's not a bad way to write." He walked over to Kalli and gave her a hug.

"Thanks, Coby, you really know how to pick them," Kalli said. "This typewriter looks like something Mom used to have. It's amazing. Thank you."

Shaking her head, Mom put the ice cream in the freezer next to the other pint. "I barely remember typewriters," she said, focusing her attention on the other pint. "So who's the ice cream bandit?"

Everyone quickly found a place around the table, which was already set. Wasting no time, Coby grabbed his mother's and sister's hands. They bowed their heads, and he gave thanks and blessed the food.

The bowl of mashed potatoes was still steaming. "Everything is perfect, Mom. Thank you," said Coby, proceeding to overload his plate. He helped himself to two rolls, a huge helping of mashed potatoes, a large piece of beef, and very few roasted vegetables.

Kalli was watching Coby, but she didn't care about leftovers. Just glad to have her brother home, she nodded in agreement with Coby.

The typewriter was center stage on Kalli's desk in the family room. She kept looking at it and could hardly wait to start writing. The condo had an open concept floor plan with the kitchen in the center. She was facing the front door, where Sid had sat earlier, and her desk was close to the television on an adjacent wall.

"So who is the ice cream bandit?" asked her mother once again.

Kalli was not sure if this was the right time, but it was an opportunity to get their collective thoughts. "Sid. He used to work with me, and now he wants me to go to New York with him for fun. He already bought the tickets and booked the rooms. We've been friends for a long time, but I'm not sure how complicated it will be."

Normally her family would hardly know her whereabouts, but since the accident there seemed to be a new level of accountability. "He has four extra tickets for the play," Kalli added, "in case anyone from our office wants to go. I'm sure there will be some takers."

The sound of choking filled the air as Coby motioned that he would be all right. "I've been wanting to go to New York and see a play," he said. "Can I get two of those tickets?"

That brought another level of questions to his mother's mind. Family dinners, one of the highlights of her daily life, were about to get even more interesting. She stayed informed about most things that went on in her children's lives, and things were much better than in the past. Coby told her about almost everything that concerned him. Penny kept more to herself, but she'd been opening up slowly. Kalli was a mystery, but her life had changed a lot, and she was still trying to figure herself out.

"So let's start with Coby," said their mother. "Coby, why two tickets?"

Coby took another bite of prime rib and said, "I don't know, Mom. Maybe I have someone I would like to take with me." Laughing, he said, "Kalli, you could stay with my friend and I could stay with Sid. I remember meeting Sid a couple of times, and I like him." Meanwhile his mother was obviously not pleased that she didn't know the "someone" he was dating.

The last slice of prime rib would go to Kalli. "I don't need anyone to stay with me. I'll be fine, or do you want me to get to know this mystery person?" Her brother looked up sheepishly. "Really, Coby?" said Kalli. "Et tu? Is someone now going to steal my brother's love from me?" She stuck her fork in another bite of prime rib and waited for his reply.

Coby looked for another slice of beef, but found none. A couple of slices were in the kitchen, covered with foil. Kalli had hoped to have enough leftovers for the next day. *Please don't get my leftovers off of the stove, mom.*

His mother rose from the table, took the leftover prime rib from the stovetop, and served Coby. "Can I have that last slice for tomorrow?" he asked. "It's not betrayal, Kalli. There's enough of me to go around. And I hope that by then, she and I will have settled our differences."

Kalli gestured to her mother to put the piece of prime rib on her own plate, but Coby shook his head. Mom got a steak knife, put a third of the slice on Kalli's plate, and wrapped the rest, along with other sides, on a plate for Coby to take with him. Kalli was hoping he would forget.

Trying not to be bothered by it, their mom asked, "So you have differences? Is that because you're leaving for Lebanon in a few months? I can see how that might be hard on a relationship."

The dining room table at which they sat was modern, snug, and not really meant for family dinners. Kalli rested her elbows on the table and nearly climbed into Coby's lap. He knew that she was determined to get to the bottom of this. It was a family trait, but he would remain strong.

"So who is she? Is she in the military?" asked Kalli. "If we're going to be roomies, I need to know her name, at least. After all, I already know I'm going to hate her."

Kalli was joking, but Coby looked up like she had guessed it.

"I *am* going to hate her?" Kalli asked. "No, it can't be. Coby, is it Sadie? It makes sense now, but you cannot be serious! Of all people, it can't be her. Granted, with her looks, she could be on the front of a magazine, but who would want to read it?"

Coby shook his head and gave her a look of warning, but Kalli continued anyway. "Magazines are an easy read, but are you truly satisfied afterward?" She paused and thought about how much she did not like this relationship and Sadie in general.

Kalli's mom hadn't seen such a sad expression on her

daughter's face since Kalli was three years old, and she would swear that a temper tantrum could follow.

"Enough, Kalli," Coby warned her. "No words, or be wise about what you say next." He sounded like their mother.

The serving dishes were empty. Mom started to clear the table, agreeing with Coby that Kalli should be quiet. "So who's ready for dessert?" she asked. "We have ice cream and fruit parfaits with yogurt and granola. You could have a fruit parfait for breakfast tomorrow, if you don't want a healthy dessert tonight." She knew there was no way to break the tension. "It's nice that Coby has a girlfriend. I'm sure she's great." She was secretly hoping that Sadie, whoever she was, would be able to change his mind about going to Beirut.

Mom wanted what was best for her children, and that meant she needed to step back from their lives from time to time and trust in God's plan instead of her own. She needed to trust their decisions and not interfere. She would be praying fervently, but not for Coby's answer to change. Instead, she prayed to be more accepting and trusting that God would keep him safe. It was never easy being Mom.

The ice cream was easy to get to in the freezer, next to the frozen pizza and vegetables. Mom reached in and grabbed it with one hand.

"I think I'll pass, Mom. I'd rather have something with more substance!" said Kalli. She was referring to Sadie, and everyone knew it. During this season in her life, Kalli would seldom pass on her favorite ice cream. Her mom and brother didn't know that she had already eaten a scoop of her favorite ice cream earlier and planned on indulging again as soon as they left.

Coby's chair slid across the floor as he stood and squinted at his sister. "You are a child, and I'm taking Sadie's side on this one. You need to learn to get along and play nice. She may not be your cup of tea, but she's definitely mine. I'm offering something nice. You'll have a little extra help if you need it and someone with whom to talk about woman stuff. It seems like a win-win to me."

Kalli *could* use the extra help if none of her other friends went along. She was pretty sure they would, but just in case, Sadie wouldn't think twice about helping her get dressed and ready. Kalli pushed her chair out of the kitchen and into the living area. "But what if I ask her about the weather?" she asked.

Coby shook his head again and grabbed his jacket.

Kalli said, "Don't go, Coby. I'll be good, and I will think about your offer and see if Sid has some extra tickets. It will be fun. You and I together before you head out for Lebanon." She wanted to say that Sadie was not that bad, but she just couldn't bring herself to do it.

Mom was excited about the trip they were planning to New York, but she wondered about everyone else who was going.

After everyone left that night, Kalli decided to call Sid instead of waiting for his call. She knew his number by heart, since she must have dialed it a thousand times for work and occasionally for an after-work get-together.

Sid worked from home more than she had, since much of his client base required travel. Without fail, he often would have to jet out for one of his clients or a potential client. It was easier for management to keep up with him if they knew he was accessible at one or the other location, and not necessarily rooming in one of their office buildings, which Kalli had done a lot for meetings.

Sid's home office was hidden within another room of his house. It was geeked out with good ventilation but no windows or natural light. A big screen and desk sat in the middle of the room, and a couple of smaller screens were connected to one or two computers. Laughing to herself, Kalli was sure that Sid might have also been a gamer or perhaps an undercover agent.

Just as Kalli called Sid on her cell phone, her video screen showed a call coming in from Coby. "Did you talk with Sid?" asked Coby. Kalli looked at her watch and then at her phone, which indicated that Sid had answered. "Hey, Sid, I have my brother on the other line. He and Sadie, his girlfriend"—she looked at Coby and nodded—"would like two of the tickets."

Coby paused and then told Kalli that he wasn't sure about Sadie yet, but that he'd like the other ticket just in case.

Kalli said, "Sid, Coby also wants to share a room with you. Then his girlfriend would stay with me, which may be a little weird."

Sid was quick to get the backstory. Coby was looking out for his little sister and wanted to get to know him. Sid liked Coby and didn't mind sharing his room. Also there was a good chance that they would be the only ones going, and Kalli would not back out if her brother was on board. So yes, Sid would be glad for the company.

When the video chat button on Sid's phone appeared,

he chose to accept. Kalli was grinning from ear to ear, which he found confusing, but he politely smiled back. Then she held up the phone next to the video screen, and Sid said, "Hi, Coby. It's been awhile. How've you been?" Coby responded in kind and told Sid that he remembered meeting him some time back.

Sid said, "Yeah, I still have two extra tickets, and it would be great to have another couple along. I'm not sure who else is going. I've reserved a couple of hotel rooms, and I can send you that information." He hoped that Kalli did not take that "couple" mention the wrong way.

But Kalli was excited to be going anywhere other than therapy. New York with her brother and Sid? She decided not to object—as long as it wasn't a date.

The screen now was tilted, as Kalli was looking at her typewriter again and then at her watch. *Today has been a good day,* Kalli thought.

Coby was looking at an almost upside-down Sid as they both tried to ignore the awkwardness of being phone to video. "Thanks, man. I appreciate it," said Coby. "I'll get the cost, your flight information, and the rest via text. I hope that we can catch the same flight. Also, not to put you out, but if you don't mind, I was thinking we could share a hotel room."

Sid hated sharing his hotel room, but he was obliged to Coby for going. Otherwise Kalli might have backed out. As the phone tilted straight, Sid said, "Great idea to share the cost. Kalli had said you would be with me and Sadie would be with her. Also, I'm having some guys over to watch the game. Do you want to come? It's Eagles versus Redskins. Kalli, you're welcome to come too."

The phone was turned toward Kalli. "It's okay to have a guy's night. I'll pass for now," she said. "But when you decide to do the politically correct thing and invite both sexes, I'll reconsider." She quickly turned the phone back to Coby on the video screen, as Sid laughed. Sid and Coby exchanged contact information, and Coby ended the call.

Sid and Kalli continued to talk, brainstorming about some of her story ideas. She took notes as Sid extrapolated on the plot. He also had some good ideas about characters, and he told her to make sure that some character traits stick out, so the character would not be forgettable. They also strategized about some of the main characters and their roles. It seemed silly at times, but Sid assured her that it wasn't silly and that she should keep at it.

By the end of their conversation, Kalli had a few pages of notes and was ready to take it to type. Sid thought it was an awesome idea to use a typewriter instead of a computer, especially since Kalli would have fewer distractions. The typewriter had autocorrect and an SD card reader to save a digital copy. Kalli liked the idea of having a paper copy to read and make notations on, which Sid said was a good idea. He knew how to have the SD card go to Wi-Fi so she would not have to transfer it, and it would be automatically backed up. He would be over the next day to show her how, if Kalli was interested. She was.

The big yarn came to Kalli first, and then Sid followed with a smaller version. They soon said good night, but not before Kalli told Sid that she didn't know what she would do without him. Sid asked her to repeat those words—"I would not know what to do without you"—but Kalli wouldn't say it again.

Sid thought that Kalli might be warming up to him. He still could not understand why he had fallen off her grace list and she had refused to see him. Maybe someday he'd figure it out or she would just tell him, but for the time being, the tension was behind them.

Sid retrieved his pint of Dutch apple meringue from the freezer and let it sit for a few minutes before he opened it. Pulling out the client list, he read over Kalli's notes. He had asked their boss to give him Kalli's client base, instead of having it evenly distributed. He had even given up some of his old clients, though he knew he would eventually get them back. He planned on building up her client base for when she returned to work, but if she chose not to, he would still have done his due diligence.

Opening the pint of ice cream, Sid took a spoonful. It was as good as he remembered. He planned on going for an extra run that evening to work off some calories, and he hoped it wouldn't be too late by the time he finished up.

★★★

The office was cold, so Dr. Hempstead turned on the heater under his desk to warm his feet. He was glad that Kalli, Penny's sister, was doing okay, and he didn't mind taking her on as a client. Of course, Kalli did not think of herself as a client. She just needed someone to talk with from time to time.

The good doctor, as everyone in the Marshall family referred to him, took a good many notes to follow therapy for both sisters. He marveled at how God had put two distinct personalities in one family. He found Penny to be single-minded but sensible, whereas Kalli was distracted, less willing to listen, and more whimsical—but not today.

Dr. Hempstead had previously noted that Kalli was playful, a bit cantankerous, and sometimes mean-spirited. She made clever jabs at his Christian viewpoints and the behavioral approach he used with Penny. He considered it to be more cognitive than behavioral, but Kalli had issues with both approaches to counseling. Sometimes she would call just to harass him or if she had questions about Christianity in general. The good doctor was never annoyed, but he always reminded her that she would be billed for the session regardless of the subject matter.

Then Kalli was usually able to identify some point of pain in her life, and they would work things out. He gave her exercises that she did not always agree with, but he called them mental therapy, so she did them whether or not she thought they would help. The good doctor did not grow on Kalli as he had on Penny. In Kalli's opinion, he was no father figure, but rather an archetype of everything that was wrong in the world, like her mom was at times.

The good doctor's phone rang just as he took out his file on Kalli and placed it on the desk. "Hello, Ms. Marshall, how are you doing today? I'm always glad to hear from you," he said. He opened her file to review several verses with little emoticons next to them, verses that Kalli had referenced in previous sessions.

The first was John 1:11–13: "He came to His own, and His own did not receive Him. But to all who did receive Him, to those who believed in His name, He gave the right to become children of God—children born not of blood, nor of the desire or will of man, but born of God."

Kalli looked at the phone in disbelief, thinking, *You're glad to hear from me?* "I had a little time on my hands before therapy, so I thought that I'd call to ask if you have time for a session. Do you?" She paused and looked down at the notebook containing some of her story ideas. Underlined twice was the word *naive*. The good doctor would always make time for Kalli until the sessions were no longer needed.

Dr. Hempstead readily agreed to the impromptu session and reminded Kalli that the session was billable. The heater on the floor beside his feet rattled, which happened when it got too hot. He reached down and turned it off.

Kalli looked at some other notes she had written down with numbers. "Yeah, sure, I know. I don't know how many sessions I have left this year. Maybe ten or more before the insurance runs out, and then it renews and I should have twenty-one more." Kalli was enthusiastically writing things down.

Kalli pulled her mother's Bible from underneath *Out of the Hidden Darkness* and the other books stacked on the table in front of her. She turned to chapter one of Genesis, at the beginning of the Bible, flipping the pages forward and then backward. "So in the beginning," Kalli started to read and then stopped. "The children to whom I read believe that every story in the Bible, starting with 'In the beginning,' is true. But I don't understand that kind of faith, logic, or science. Do you?"

Kalli had no malicious intent. She just wanted to know what was true. "Dr. Hempstead, I'm sure Penny has told you about Coby, our brother. He told me that if I'm interested in understanding the Bible, I should start with John. But I want to start at the beginning where it all began, if that's okay with you."

Chapter 15

Where to Begin Again

The maître'd spoke French to the couple entering the restaurant, asking if they preferred a window table or booth. Sadie answered in French and looked to Coby, who was also fluent in French, for his approval. The booth by the window, tucked away in the corner of the French restaurant, was fine, but Coby pointed to a vacant table being cleaned by a busboy. The maître'd was not pleased, but he showed them to the table anyway. The table was quickly cleaned, and they were seated opposite each other.

Sadie laughed after the maître'd handed them menus and left. She was putting on airs and thought it was funny that Coby followed suit. They always had fun going out together. Sadie was an extrovert and loved getting to know new people. Coby had a general interest in people, but not like Sadie. She usually had about a thousand questions for anyone with whom they came in contact, and Coby would follow up with a few questions of his own. People could not escape them, although many tried.

Coby was not so bad. He generally stuck to the "Where are you from?" questions, but Sadie always wanted to know more about people. "Where are you from?" only got the conversation started, and "Where were you born?" usually ended it.

The empty silence was unbearable for Coby. Sadie typically had a thousand things stored up to tell him when she saw him in person, but now she just blankly stared at him and the menu. Their laughter had faded, and a somberness filled the air.

Sadie put down her menu, surveyed her surroundings, and asked, "So why here, Coby? We are going to talk about the same stuff no matter where we are, and this place is going to cost you a small fortune." Normally Sadie would have appreciated the gesture, but she had already written off their relationship. "I can't be with someone who's going to be away for years. It's just too hard. I don't have that kind of personality." Coby reached over the table and grabbed her hand, but she pulled it away.

The maître'd whispered something in the ear of their waiter, who then approached their table with a bottle of wine. When Coby declined the wine, the waiter poured water for them.

"Sadie, I can't do this again. I don't know how to begin again without you. Tell me what you want from me, and we'll be done with it." Coby placed his napkin on his lap.

In no time at all, Sadie's eyes welled up with tears. The waiter placed bread between them, but Sadie quickly moved it aside and said, "That's just it. I'm not going to tell you what you need to do for me. I'm going to be okay, and so will you. I trust God for that much. It just sucks, that's all."

The waiter returned to the front of the restaurant, impatiently waiting for Coby to close his menu, but then Sadie opened hers again and held it in front of her. If they looked down again at their menus, he would go over and suggest an appetizer. In the shadows, he waited and watched.

Coby fished for Sadie's hand, but she would not surrender it. "I was hoping we could do this together," he said. "We could go to Lebanon together. I'm not going because this is a career move of epic proportions, but because I feel that I'm being called in this direction. Get it?"

Sadie glanced down at her menu and then back up at Coby. The waiter quickly approached them, but Coby shook his head. Sadie asked, "Coby, do you know what you're saying?"

Coby's gaze was resolute. He reached across the table, grabbed her hand, and held it tight. "Yes, I want us to spend the rest of our lives together. I'm not proposing marriage right now, but I want you to know that. You decide what you want to do, and then we'll either make our plans or go our separate ways. Please come with me."

The waiter approached, but then retreated hastily when Coby again shook his head vehemently, still holding Sadie's hand.

Sadie sat quietly, neither happy nor sad. "As your wife?" she asked. Stern and unforgiving, she looked at him as if this was his last chance.

Immense relief washed over Coby. "Yes, as my wife," he said. Sadie was tall and lanky, but that did not stop her from practically leaping over the table and hugging Coby.

He could feel her wet face against his neck. He turned his head to see the other diners looking at them, but his focus came back and he cheerfully pulled Sadie away from him. "I'm not proposing, not yet anyway," he said, and she nodded enthusiastically.

★★★

The screen was idle for several seconds before the next player logged on. "Sid, are you ready?" asked Jedi, which was not his real name. Jedi was an old friend of Sid's, and his player name stemmed from action hero figures that they used to play with as young kids. Sid knew that Jedi was not asking him about the game, but rather about the coming weekend and their trip together.

The game began. Several mutants from the outside forest attacked them from each side, but they were overly eager to slaughter them with every move. "I already told you that I won't be able to make it this weekend. I've got other plans," said Sid. Jedi uttered some choice words, not for Sid but for their opponents. Sid looked up at the top of his screen and then back down.

The water started to rise onto the bridge as they approached the river. "Did you want to swim or take our chances?" asked Jedi, and he dove into the water. "No, you said that you *might* have other plans. I was hoping that *might* was reflective of a pivotal decision. After all, we've gone on this crusade for the last two years. You can't say the medieval stuff has worn off, because it's timeless."

The bridge was flooded, and Sid had waited too long. Jedi almost made it to the other side before he died. Sid climbed a tree and noticed a boat tied to another tree downstream. He climbed down, let the tide carry him to the boat, and climbed in. He began rowing farther downstream and across to the other side. Meanwhile Jedi had regenerated next to a similar boat, which he climbed into and started rowing to the other side of the river.

When Sid's boat washed ashore, he scrambled onto the beach. He waited patiently for his teammate to get across the river so they could fight an incoming enemy or find a place to hide while the enemy marched past their location. "No, I think I was over the festival last year when it was just the two of us," he replied. "It seemed repetitive."

Jedi's small boat finally debarked. "Does Kalli have anything to do with you ditching me this weekend? You know I don't want to go by myself. You do know how much you mean to me, right?"

Two screens flickered brightly, which would have been distracting for a non-gamer. "Kalli and I aren't dating," said Sid. "I'm having some people over to watch the game, including her brother. You can come too, if you want."

As Jedi clambered toward the shore, Sid asked, "Hide?" They waited behind some nearby bushes as the army of half fly and half silver-tongued serpents flew and walked by, cutting down everything in their path. They were worth points, but they didn't feed into the goal of getting to the next level and slaying one of the many queens. That would give Sid and Jedi a short reprieve before beginning the quest of rescuing the children.

"I'm hurt," said Jedi. Sid immediately looked at his friend's health rating level and realized he was talking about the festival. Jedi dodged out of view of one of the last remaining alien beings.

Sid said, "Seriously, you can't have been looking forward to it that much. Just come over and watch the game with us, Panthers versus Redskins. It should be good, although the main quarterback is out for the season." Then Sid gulped and said, "Or is it that other thing?"

There was silence and then radio chatter from another game that Sid wanted to play. Looking at the smaller screen, he grabbed his other keyboard and logged off.

"I don't know what you see in her and not in me," said Jedi. "She's not your type at all, especially now. There are limitations to what you can expect, as you know. She's disabled, and you ... Well, you love the outdoors, and you're always on the go." Jedi and Sid had been friends since they were kids, so Jedi knew Sid well.

The wide path they had been traveling narrowed, and they took turns walking in front. The forest was now shadowy as the thickness of the brush and the darkness increased, and utter doom loomed in the sky.

Sid said, "It's my choice, and I choose Kalli if she'll have me. I've known her for a long time, and it's always been her. No one else, no matter who I was dating." He paused, thinking out loud and becoming more confident as he spoke. "Whatever she has to endure, I'll take it in stride. I'm not perfect, but I'll be there for her the best I can. I've always liked her. She's difficult, but beautiful." Sid shot his arrow into the sky against an onslaught of longhaired, winged beasts with scorpion tails. The first one was easy; it fell to the ground, only to stagger up in stubborn rebellion against defeat.

"We should have just gone back," said Jedi, jabbing at the creature with his sword. "I wish we all had a choice. You know how I feel, if you ever change your mind. I admire the challenge, but if it's ever too much ..." Jedi was about to give up his second life, as Sid partially restored him with some of his own points. The winged creatures were there to sting and torment the mortals until they had had enough and surrendered in acknowledgment of the game's master and creator.

Sid said, "Cut the crap, Jedi. Don't believe that you are predestined in that way. There is no biological evidence that suggests that you don't have a choice in who you like or don't. You have that choice, just as anyone has the choice to go in one direction or the other. It may seem at times that we can go only one way, but we have options." Sid he took his machete and chopped through the bush, forging a way onto another path.

The path was widening as their tormentors followed but stayed back. Sid and Jedi were able to walk side by side, examining objects for clues as they walked. "But there are right choices and wrong choices," said Jedi. "Just because there's a choice does not mean it's ultimately the best choice." He was pleased with his answer, but it made Sid cringe.

"Yes, a choice is a choice, no matter how you choose to color it," said Sid. "If I tried to force a puzzle piece into the wrong space, it would be obvious to me that it didn't fit, so I would choose a different piece. I love you like a brother, Jedi, but I just don't get it."

The path was starting to narrow again. Jedi said, "It's just harder for me. I know what makes me happiest. Do you want me to be happy? I want that for you."

Surrender was not an option, but the new enemy was relentless. "I'm not sure whether happiness is the end game or just part of it," admitted Sid. "I think happiness has its own set of rules. As children, cookies, cake, and sweets make us happy, but in the end they rob us of our health."

There was a small light in the distance. "Should we keep going until the path ends or go toward the light?" asked Jedi, already starting to veer off path. "I don't think we can decide the right or wrong kind of happiness for each other."

Sid stayed the course, so Jedi came back to the original path. "With that being said, we've known each other since we were young, so I'm not sure why we're having this conversation," said Sid. "You should just be happy for me, that I found someone with whom I'm interested in pursuing a relationship." Sid paused and then said in a soft, gentle voice, "I do think you are persuing the wrong kind of happiness."

Jedi had no more words for Sid, who had no more thoughts on the subject. They continued to play, but it was hard for them to talk about anything other than the game at hand.

★★★

The more Kalli thought about New York, the more excited she got. She was also relieved that the thought of spending time with Sadie no longer made her physically ill, although she still felt queasy when she thought of Sadie and Coby together.

Sadie had gotten tips from Coby about how *not* to get on Kalli's nerves, but everything he told her was basically useless. Kalli would just find some other irritating trait to concentrate on. Coby told Sadie that if she would be herself and stop tiptoeing around Kalli, eventually his sister would respect her. Meanwhile Sadie made a list of things *not* to do if she truly wanted to win Kalli over.

Sadie and the kids came to Kalli's door. Since they took some time off for Thanksgiving, she hadn't seen any of them for a while, and soon they'd be taking a Christmas break. As they entered the condo, they each gave Kalli a hug and a small Christmas gift that she placed on her kitchen table. Some gifts were ornaments, and others were mini homemade bags filled with potpourri, candy, or chewing gum. Yet other gifts were pictures—mostly favorite Bible verses with the kid's name underneath—that Sadie had put into frames. Kalli was not much for giving Christmas gifts or other sentimental notions, and it had been a while. But for the moment, it seemed like the Christmases of old that could fill a child with faith and hope.

The children told Kalli to read fast, since they had a play they wanted to perform. They did not have costumes or a manger, but she knew it was the Nativity story of Christ's birth. The children really wanted Kalli to believe in Jesus. Even though she never expressed her opinion one way or the other, somehow they just knew.

It was the last chapter of their book. They would start the first chapter of the next book by the same author if they had time, but that was unlikely because of the seasonal festivities that Kalli and Sadie had planned. The children were told to get their cookies and hot cider with cinnamon sticks, and then go and sit in their usual spots.

"Really, Ms. Sadie and Ms. Kalli, you outdid yourselves this year. Merry Christmas!" said Ellie as she picked out her two Christmas cookies. The other kids agreed. Kalli laughed and Sadie rolled her eyes. Kalli was warm, so she asked Dwight to open the sliding glass door a crack to let in some air. He gladly did so and returned to his spot on the floor.

Kalli said, "As you remember, some of the main characters had become trapped, like the king himself. The king was the keeper whom they first met but had not recognized, and the evil queen was the person who stood behind the king. The king had warned them to leave, but they pursued the mission, not recognizing him as the king. Now, after several weeks, this is where we left off in the story." The rest of the story was read quickly, and the children applauded.

Then they assembled swiftly and took their positions for the Nativity scene. They explained that the fact that Mary and Joseph rode in on a donkey did not mean that the family was poor; in fact, it may have been a sign of royalty. The gifts that were given may have supported Jesus's ministry as the Son of God. The stars in the sky had been guiding the magi and the shepherds for years, and baby Jesus might have been more than a year old when everyone arrived to honor their king. There really was not much play acting, but rather an explanation of facts.

Tina wanted to know if Kalli had any questions. "No," said Kalli, "but the play was very well done."

Ellie asked shyly, "So you understand that Jesus came as God and died for everyone's sins? He rose again from the grave!"

Sadie looked at Kalli wide-eyed. Realizing that she was part of an ambush, Kalli glared at Sadie, who shrugged. Kalli pointed to the table with her gifts for them, but they did not move as Tina was steering Kalli down.

"Yes, but that is a personal decision, isn't it?" asked Kalli.

Sadie lowered her head, Tina grinned brilliantly, and the children looked at each other. "Choose to be forgiven," said Tina, "forever and ever. No one will ever love you as much as Jesus, although sometimes life gets hard." Tina had lost her father in combat. "You are precious to Him alone," she added, and the other children agreed. Ellie stood beside Tina and took a bow for her performance. "Jesus loves me, this I know, for the Bible tells me so. That was my favorite song when I was little," said Tina. "Just believe."

Sadie stood up, patted Ellie and Tina on the back, and pointed to the presents. She asked Tina and Arthur to help hand them out to everyone else, and then they had time for one game.

Sadie apologized, but Kalli said, "For what? They're just children. What do they know? They're regurgitating what they have been taught."

Sadie said, "No, not regurgitating, but expressing

the hope that they have inside their hearts. After all, it's Christmas."

"But I am precious to Him alone? What does that mean?" asked Kalli. "Why am I not precious to the entire universe?" She was trying to get a rise out of Sadie.

Sadie laughed and said, "I suppose you would be if the universe had a name, was responsible for your creation, and died on the cross so that in the end you would be with Him again." She looked at the children who had strategically laid out a plan for Kalli's salvation and wondered how they had done it. But then she realized it was not them, but the hand of God.

★★★

Fred was once again at Kalli's doorstep. He was allowed into her condominium without knocking, but as he entered, he would always ask if anyone was home. Kalli would unlock the door for him in advance, since she knew when he was scheduled to arrive. Fred had been driving her to and from her therapy appointments, along with other errands, for several months, so they were now on more familiar terms.

He would have helped himself to a beer, but there were none—which was good since Kalli would have fired him on the spot. Fred spotted a bottle of wine, but knew their relationship was not yet at the stage where he could pour himself a glass. *Give it a year,* he thought, assuming he did not move on to something else. He made himself comfortable on the couch and looked around at all the expensive furniture. He also studied her German clock and wondered how much it was worth.

Kalli had been going out a great deal more, especially during the holidays, and Fred was always there to drive. She felt obliged to show her appreciation for that. "Hey, my gift to you is that you don't have to tip me for the holidays," said Fred, chuckling as he hoisted his legs onto the coffee table.

Kalli *never* tipped, but Fred had already included that in his fare. "Thanks," she replied sarcastically as she emerged from her bedroom and handed him a Christmas card with a fifty-dollar Visa card. She smiled as if that was the best gift in the world. His gift of not tipping was fine too, since she had no expectations about gift giving. She had often wished that Christmas was not a thing, just for that reason of gift giving alone. As far as tipping was concerned, she chose to do it on occasion.

Besides, she was charged plenty for Fred's service. The notion that he discounted her fare because he was her sole driver was a lie, but she had no idea since it fell within the range of limousine drivers, which she thought to be accurate. Kalli did not know what to tip, so she didn't. Also, she knew that she was paying three times a normal fare just because she was in a wheelchair and Fred knew what to expect. Fred would help her into the car and store her portable chair for a lot of money. *Big deal*, she thought.

The idea of having her own wheels had become more and more enticing, even if the speed of the vehicle was less than that of a normal car. The Solo could be used only for short distances since it was electric. She would never have to put gas in it, but she would have to keep it charged. Not a problem, she thought, since there were several charging stations outside her condominium for electric vehicles.

The fact that her car would be slow was okay with Kalli. Since her accident, she had been in no hurry to get behind the wheel of a regular car. The Solo was less intimidating and functioned more like a golf cart. She would have to take a lot of side roads, since it could not go the speed of the interstate highway, but it would be sweet. Everything close by where she lived was convenient and off the main thoroughfare. Kalli would miss Fred, but she could have him over from time to time. Then she decided that she would miss him only temporarily, so it was no big deal.

"Thank you," said Fred. "You have no idea how much this means to me." *Actually it means nothing*, he thought, looking at an expensive piece of abstract art hanging on one wall. But if he needed more, he would just tell her that his fare was going up and hope that she wouldn't find another driver.

Something in his gut told him that their relationship could soon be coming to an end anyway, which meant it was time to move on to something else. Kalli, too, wondered where Fred would be the next Christmas and if he would still be her driver. If she could find another mode of transportation, she would be more independent and happier, and Fred could go back to driving other people around.

Fred, however, had other plans. He had been casing her place from the very beginning. He had picked her up from her apartment, driven her to her destination, and then doubled back and broken into her home. He had been prepared to tell anyone who caught him that he was retrieving something for Kalli, since he would be picking her up and returning with her shortly, but no one had asked any questions.

The cigarette butt that Fred had discarded in Kalli's yard hadn't gone unnoticed, but what did he care? His work had been accomplished. He now knew the layout of the apartment, grounds, and complex. Most people who noticed him thought that he lived there, since he was there so frequently. Fred was always careful not to talk to anyone, so he had no ties to anybody at the complex other than Kalli.

All the security cameras could easily be avoided by sticking close to the building, and if there were any other hidden camera, he'd be dressed for the occasion. Not in a sweatshirt with a hoodie, but in a ball cap, sunglasses, and jacket similar to that of another tenant. Actually it would be similar to two other tenants, he told himself.

★★★

Sid had set up a Wi-Fi SD card inside Kalli's typewriter, which connected to a network with its own group share. As long as it was active, she could share and download documents as if the typewriter had built-in Wi-Fi capabilities. Sid explained that it was safe from hackers since she wasn't storing anything in the cloud. Instead, everything was stored locally on a drive that was part of the router that she had purchased. Kalli had no idea how a router worked or how to set it up, so Sid had set it up for her.

The green light on the router flashed off and on. Sid explained that he could adjust that setting if she wanted it to be a steady green, but Kalli said, "I think it's fine if it flashes. That way I know it's working." She was pleased with the way everything was flowing. "So I can give you a password, and you can log on to my network and download my document, but that is all you can download?" asked Kali. She was worried that Sid would stumble across her financial documents and realize how broke she was.

The typewriter turned off and on again. Sid finished testing the Wi-Fi connection and was pleased to have her document on his phone. "Yeah," he said, not really paying attention. "Hey, this is really good. You've done some editing, and it reads even better than when we worked on it together." He kept reading and then, sounding a bit surprised, said, "I think you have some talent."

Kalli bumped her chair against his and said, "So are you going to answer me? Can you get into all my files? Is this just a ruse so that you can snoop through my stuff?" She was trying to make light of her concern, but she really would be mortified if he tapped into her journal. She hadn't been keeping it online, but now she was thinking about doing so since she was having so much fun typing.

Sid realized that he needed to have a heart-to-heart talk with Kalli about how this technology worked. His chair slid backward across the floor as he stood up, which pushed Kalli's chair a little sideways. "So do you care for some ice cream? I'll serve and you write," he suggested. Kalli just nodded, so Sid continued, "Your question is a little open ended. If I have the password to your network, I can hack pretty much anything you have saved on your computer, though I won't. If you want to change the password to your network, I'll still be able to get to the story that you're writing." Sid stopped in front of the refrigerator and doubled back to the kitchen table.

Kalli looked up at him and grinned. "You're going to map this out for me, aren't you?" she asked. When she had technical questions at work about email filters or anything else, she would always ask Sid, but she had never understood his answer until he drew it out.

Laughing, Sid looked around and grabbed a discarded food wrapper and a pen from the countertop. Then he drew a picture of the typewriter, her router, and the outside world. "Your typewriter is not connected to anything without this orange Wi-Fi SD card to which your document is copied." Then he drew a document with wings and continued, "But then any document stored on this Wi-Fi card can go to the hard drive on this router and be shared with anyone using the password. Actually it has its own router, but for the sake of simplicity, let's just say that it goes to this hub."

The black SD card next to her typewriter seemed safest to Kalli at that moment. "I really don't mind just giving you the SD card from time to time as we collaborate on my story. What do you think?"

Knowing that she wouldn't take no for an answer, Sid shook his head and his pen flew across the paper once more. "It's not complicated, Kalli. If you write something personal such as journal entries, use the black SD card, but it won't be backed up. But you should know that your network is safe. Your router has firewalls to stop a normal hacker, who should and will have better things to hack than your typewriter. You gave me your password and I helped you set everything up, but you can always change that password. That will not affect me sharing your document, since I'll be connecting to the card almost directly." He circled a small portion of the router and the typewriter, which had an arrow pointing from a poorly drawn computer with the name *Sid* on it.

Kalli squinted at the drawing and then at Sid. She still had questions swirling about her head, but she trusted him. "Okay, if I do my journal, I'll do it on the black memory card and then stick it into my computer and back it up on that. That is, if I stop journaling by hand, which I probably won't do." Mentally processing as she talked, Kalli added, "Never mind. That's a mute point."

Sid leaned over to kiss her and then stopped himself. He wasn't used to being so close to someone he liked and having to hide it. Then he caught it and chuckled. "Did you say *mute*? Like *quiet*?"

Kalli pushed her wheelchair away from the table. As she pulled open the bottom half of the refrigerator, the freezer light came on and she saw where Sid had put the two half-pints of ice cream on top. She hoped once more that he would forget his. "Yes, like the point is quieted. I get it. I will journal only with pen and paper. I just realized I'm more comfortable that way," she said loudly, as if she had just made a life-changing decision.

Standing close to the fridge and Kalli, Sid said, "It is moot. It's a moot point, unresolved." He reached up, grabbed two bowls, and put them on the counter. She got spoons and napkins, then leaned in and placed everything on her lap. It was their way. He was then able to take the wheelchair handles and push her forward, which previously he had not been allowed to do.

Sid recognized the scent of Kalli's hair from the office—lilac and lavender. She often would come in early with her hair still wet and leave a trail of lilac and lavender scent in the hallway to her office. He would follow the scent and tell her good morning. He became conscious that he had fallen far out of his comfort zone with Kalli, but he wouldn't trade the insecurity for anything different.

She reached back and placed her hand on his. Her head was turned just enough for him to see the glint in her eyes and her smile. It was almost like time flashed forward and he could see her older but still just as beautiful. It was oddly familiar, as though they had known each other for a lifetime. It gave him goose bumps.

The ice cream was cold in her lap. "So it's moot, because I'm going to do things my way no matter what, so there's no need for debate. But it's also mute, because we don't need to discuss it any longer and we can just be quiet," she said glibly.

Sid laughed and shrugged. He would have taken the bowls from her, but she had already set them on the table. She handed him the ice cream, and he scooped it out. He couldn't shake the thoughts that were in his head. He had a dire urge to tell her how he felt. He ate his cold ice cream while thinking things that he wanted to say but couldn't.

Neapolitan was her least favorite ice cream, but it was still ice cream. Kalli aimed a spoonful for her mouth, but it slid off and fell to the table. She swept it up with her napkin.

Looking at Kalli's lips, Sid thought, *If only I were ice*

cream. He would wait until after New York, but eventually he hoped to turn her affections from friend to boyfriend.

Kalli looked at him and realized he was somewhere else. She took an even larger spoonful of ice cream and raised it to her mouth, but this time she didn't miss.

Chapter 16

New York

The security camera box lay unopened on Kalli's countertop. She had been meaning to hook it up or ask one of the two main men in her life to help her. Kalli chided herself for being lazy and not wanting to read the instructions to do it herself. Before closing the front door behind her, she took a final look around her condo.

She had a feeling in the pit of her stomach that she was forgetting something. Suddenly she realized what it was—she was missing Fred, her driver and escort. It was still unusual for Kalli to leave her home by herself. She had gotten used to having Fred around, although he had become too comfortable with her. The necessary professionalism and respect between client and driver had been eroded.

Fred had left her company for other employment, but she had not missed him like he had warned that she would. He had wanted a raise, but she had refused to pay him anything more than their original agreement. She was not the least bit heartbroken; in fact, she had taken it as validation that she was ready to be an independent driver. She had put in an order for a Solo, which would ship within the next three months, but for now her mom was helping her.

Kalli waved at her mom, who had just pulled up and parked next to the ramp. "How are you, my dear?" asked Mom, getting out and helping Kalli into the van.

Kalli lifted herself onto the seat and buckled herself in. "I'm doing well, Mom. I don't resent spending time with you like I did before the accident. Thank you for the lift." Mom just nodded, and Kalli continued, "I wrote down a list of items that I need for our New York trip. If you want to come with us, I don't think anyone would mind. It's not like any of my old friends are coming. I've been pretty much dissed by them."

A white Mercedes van pulled up behind them. Mom was already in the front seat and had just pulled her favorite Ray-Ban Wayfarers out of the sunglasses holder between the two sun visors. Looking at her rearview mirror, she said, "No, I thought about it. More time with two of my favorite children? But alas, I have other plans. Do you know who that is behind us?"

Kalli pulled out her phone and took a picture of the van behind them. She enlarged the picture and studied the driver. "No, nobody I've seen before now. Why do you ask?"

The driver of the van honked to let them know Mom needed to move. "The driver looks a little suspicious," said Mom. "Ball cap, sunglasses, windows tinted darker than allowed in this state, out-of-state tags, and now they're impatiently honking. If they were interested in being in this space, they should already have parked. Unless they're delivering something, in which case that's not the vehicle they should be driving—or even able to afford."

Kalli had already deleted the picture. "You sound like Coby. Please take off your spy hat, put on your chauffeur cap, and drive." Kalli liked to tease her mom, but she was being serious too. She hated wasting time and energy on things she thought to be worthless.

Continuing to stare at the impetuous driver behind her, Mom put her car in gear and slowly pulled forward.

Incognito, Fred put his car in gear and followed suit. After parking, he could not help laughing. Nobody, including Kalli or her mom, would recognize him as someone who was not supposed to be there. He quickly pulled a clearly marked moving box from the van, stopping briefly a few feet from the van so Mom could see what he was carrying.

Mom looked back at him and smiled. "Oh, Kalli, it looks like you're going to have a new neighbor—impatient but moderately handsome, although it's hard to tell for sure."

Looking in the rearview mirror, Kalli quickly took a few more snapshots of the man so she could get a closer view. She studied her phone and said, with a chuckle, "Not so handsome. He's rather skinny and looks a little rough around the edges. He must be the previously pending sale on the second floor ... But I thought that was a family of three and still pending." She studied the pictures a little closer and decided to hang on to them for a bit.

Fred carried the box to Kalli's front door, set it down on the concrete, and pulled his keys out of his pocket. The next-door neighbor opened her door and stuck her head out. She waved to him as she retrieved a package from outside her door, and Fred politely waved back. *This is too easy,* he thought.

Taking out his phone, he scanned for Bluetooth devices. A few cameras from some of the other condos registered a few hundred feet away, but nothing from Kalli's condo. He let himself in, picking up his box and setting it on the kitchen table. He noticed the cameras, uninstalled and still in their unopened boxes, on the kitchen counter. *Just in time*, he thought.

Kalli's video device suddenly announced a call from Coby. Fred hit *decline*, took a can of red spray paint from his box, and sprayed the screen.

Wondering why Kalli had declined his call, Coby decided to drop in on Kalli's video device. He saw mostly red and heard a man apparently talking to himself: "This is like candy. Kalli should've never let me go. I would've probably become quite close to her if she had let me." Hearing those words, Coby thought, *Sid. That has to be Sid.*

Coby recorded the video and chat on his phone, but he still couldn't make out the voice. It had to be Sid, but that was really out of character for him. Who else could it be? Continuing to listen, Coby put himself on mute and called the police on the other line.

Kalli was enjoying her time with her mother in the car. She told her about her Solo and how she would be an independent driver soon. They had just pulled into a parking space directly in front of LMs when she received a phone call from Sid. "Yeah, Sid. No, yeah. Say that again," said Kalli. Mom was still talking to her, but Kalli motioned for her mom to be quiet. Then she placed the phone on the dashboard, and she and her mom heard Sid's voice coming from the speaker.

"Coby called me after texting me while he was watching and listening to some guy ransack your condo," Sid explained. "Coby's on the phone with the police right now, and they are on their way to your condo." He was looking at his phone and checking his texts.

Kalli and her mother exchanged looks, and Mom said angrily, "The clock. I hope he doesn't get away with the clock. In fact, I hope he doesn't get away at all." She grabbed Kalli's hand, which her daughter allowed, although she took no comfort in it.

Kalli gazed momentarily at Mom and the phone, and then she let them have it. Words came from Kalli's mouth that neither Sid nor her mother had ever heard. "Take me back, Mom. I want to be there when they arrest him," she said, muttering something that they interpreted as "dirty bastard." Mom started her car as Sid and Kalli continued to talk.

Sid said, "I just got a text from Coby. They've already apprehended the culprit. Mystery solved, Coby writes. It was the chauffeur. Coby had thought it was me, so he had texted and then called me. It was some stuff the chauffeur said about wanting to be close to you." Sid realized his mistake immediately, but it was already out there. And anyway, everyone except for Kalli would have already guessed his feelings for her.

Thankfully Kalli was only half listening as she thumbed through Coby's texts: "Are you all right? Don't go home. I love you, Sis." His last text said, "We got him."

Kalli exclaimed, "They have him! Yay! They got Fred. I can't believe he would do that to me. It's because I didn't tip him, not because I wasn't close to him. Who said that? I bet it was Fred who left my patio door open that day when I sent Mom—for reasons unknown to her—to check out my condo. Remember, you and Coby got angry with me for not thinking of others!" Then glancing at her silent mother's white face and pursed lips, Kalli added, "Oh."

"You did that?" asked Sid, followed by a long pause. "I'll meet you and your mother at your place." With that, he ended the call.

★★★

The half-eaten but trendy pair of jeans lay on the white duvet, next to her even more stylish brown ankle boots, which were placed neatly on top of her beige fisherman's sweater. Her other outfits were already packed in her blue suitcase. This would be the first outfit that she would wear, on the plane and during her first day in New York. She planned to wear a shirt under her sweater so that she wouldn't be too hot or cold on the plane. The other outfits were part of her cold-weather wardrobe strategy, which in some cases included up to four layers of clothing. Even so, she was a little anxious that she might not have packed correctly.

Within hours she would be on a plane to JFK with Sid, Sadie, and Coby. This still felt a little weird for her, since Coby was really the only one with whom she definitely wanted to spend time on their New York trip. Everyone else could be fun, but she was not sure yet. Kalli would trust Coby with her life, but everyone else was still growing on her—like fungi, thought Kalli. Sid was a good fungus, like a special kind of expensive mushroom. Sadie, on the other hand, was a different kind of fungus. Kalli wasn't really sure where Sadie fit in the fungi world, except that she was no longer a black mold. Kalli laughed to herself and thought, *Yes, fungi among us.*

Kalli heard the front door open and shut. Sid called out her name, like he had on occasion when picking her up for a business trips. She yelled back, "In the bedroom, if you don't mind." She was hoping to get some help with her suitcase.

Kalli was overcome by memories ... She had usually been running late. If they had planned to meet at the gate, Sid would be waiting there and Kalli would show up just in time to board. But if she persuaded him to swing by and pick her up, which at first he resented, she would still be in the midst of dressing and packing when he got there. Garments would be strewn across the bed, not neatly packed in her valise. Kalli invariably would be trying on new shoes. She always wanted to be comfortable, but she would slip her tiny feet into a pair of high heels just because they perfectly matched her skirt, top, and handbag. In fact, those high heels would often be the same brand as her bag—Prada, or a less expensive but well-known brand. But today, it was all about comfort.

"Are you ready?" Sid asked. Kalli zipped up her suitcase and left it on her bed for him to carry out. The suitcase was much larger than what he had seen her use previously, but still not unusually large for a woman going on a trip. Kalli had forgotten how many times he had found her still going through her closet. He would patiently wait, making jokes and telling stories. And she would tell him that he needed to be quiet or she would never finish packing.

For Kalli, the thought of being so different from before the accident felt like an upset stomach. "Yeah, Sid, I'm ready," she said. "Packed and ready for our grand adventure in New York."

Sid studied her quietly for a moment. Then he picked up the oversized bag and humorously and slowly dragged it across the floor.

Knowing that she had overpacked, Kalli said, "It has a pull-out handle like normal suitcases." She chuckled briefly, but for the moment she was still lost in memories.

"I like the new you better," said Sid. Kalli cocked her head as if to say, *How the hell did you know?* A delicate smile, which he had never seen before, crossed her face. *I'm going to marry that smile*, he said to himself. "Shall we?" he asked, and Kalli nodded.

The plane touched down at JFK. They had opted for an economy upgrade that gave them plenty of leg room. "We're here! I know that I'm stating the obvious—but New York, here we come!" said Sadie, looking at Kalli.

Kalli had been about to say the same thing, but without so much enthusiasm. It sounded so dumb coming from Sadie's lips that she was glad Sadie had said it first.

The song "New York, New York" came into both Coby and Sadie's minds. Sadly, Sadie knew the melody would not be welcomed, but she hummed it under her breath anyway. She would definitely pick up some souvenirs, including an "I Love New York" T-shirt. She could hardly believe she was in the Big Apple at last.

As the plane taxied more slowly, Kalli's mind was on exiting. She had never done that in a wheelchair, but she had tried to prepare herself. She knew there would be an attendant with a second wheelchair waiting outside the plane, and from that point it became simpler. She tried not to look nervous.

Coby squeezed Sadie's hand twice: first, for her obvious excitement, and second, because she was staring at Kalli and probably wondering how this would work. Sadie had called the airline and hotel to ask about wheelchair accessibility, and she had learned that it was hard for someone with a disability to get around without assistance from other people. Although she remained a little anxious, since this was new ground for her, she wasn't going to let it overcome the excitement of being in New York.

The plane was now at a complete stop. Sadie pulled her hand from under Coby's and placed it on top of his. They locked eyes, and she grinned. If they ever split up, it would not be for lack of communication. Then the scary thought of losing Coby was quickly replaced as Sadie placed all things in the hands of the Almighty, trusting His will more than her own.

They were able to get off the plane with little effort, after waiting for the other passengers to exit. Kalli was not as annoyed as she had anticipated with her brother's new friend, Sadie, who walked beside her as Coby pushed the chair. Sid walked behind the small group, thinking that they were engaging and fun. He felt that he was experiencing a life transition, though he wasn't sure how all the people or pieces quite fit.

Their self-automated car was waiting on the other side of Podium Drive, where the conductor of sorts made sure everyone safely exited and entered their vehicles. These driverless cars could be found only in certain areas of New York, and JFK Airport was the first hub for this type of transit.

"So I thought this would be fun!" said Sid. "What do you think?" Nobody spoke up to state the obvious. Risk aside, as Sadie was thinking, it was soon to be the norm.

The conductor, John, asked if they smoked or vaped, which Sadie thought was an odd question. But then, upon catching a faint scent of skunk, she raised her eyebrows and said in a stern voice, "No, we don't, nor would we want to ride in a vehicle that smelled, you know, of smoke." Coby laughed, and John showed them to a less contaminated vehicle. It was not illegal to own certain types of smokes, but a person could be arrested for growing, trading, buying, or selling them. Coby laughed again at that loophole, which should have been considered an oversight.

Sid signed for the vehicle, but then he immediately dropped the keys into Coby's hand. "Do you mind?" he asked. "I thought I'd sit in back with Kalli and point out the sights on the way to the hotel."

Coby checked to make sure Kalli was okay with that, and she gave him a thumbs-up. He wasn't sure why his little sister was okay with Sid, but he was glad she was interested.

Horns were blowing and the air was thick, but nothing

took away from the feeling of being in a historic place for the first time. As they passed famous landmarks, everyone enjoyed Sid's narrative about New York's importance and the historical significance of certain buildings. Sadie asked Sid to speak up, and then Kalli rolled her eyes as he switched to an unnatural baritone voice.

When the car pulled up to valet parking in front of the hotel, Coby handed the keys to the attendant. The wheelchair was quickly retrieved from the back seat for Kalli, who needed no assistance in transferring herself into it. The hotel bellhop eagerly unloaded their luggage, even though everyone insisted on carrying their own bags inside, where they were politely greeted by the hotel staff. Sadie grabbed Kalli's suitcase and carried it along with her own.

Sid had reserved rooms on the eighth floor, so that they would have a good view of the Upper East Side of Manhattan. Sadie and Kalli's room was on the same side as Coby and Sid's, just as he had requested. The rooms weren't anything special except for the baskets of goodies. Sid felt both pleased and anxious as he thought about the accommodations and everything else he had planned.

Sadie flung both suitcases onto the bed closest to the window and asked, "Can you believe we're here?"

Kalli moved her suitcase to the other bed, thinking that even though she was just as excited as Sadie, she would limit herself to one stupid question per night.

"Did you want to change or go as you are?" asked Sadie.

Not such a stupid question, thought Kalli, who was already unzipping her luggage and pulling out one of her many outfits. Actually the casual dress, which went with boots, was part of another outfit. It wasn't one of the outfits that she had originally planned to wear, so it was three or four layers down, but she knew it was perfect for the evening.

Noticing a look of envy on Sadie's face, Kalli said, "I have something for you, too." Sadie was taller than her, but still a medium. Kalli pulled out a cute opal blouse by Love Sam and a skirt that was easily pulled together with the matching belt and shoes that Sadie was already wearing.

Sadie nodded and smiled, thinking that this was exactly the kind of bonding moment for which she had been waiting. Still, she knew that she would blow it if Kalli noticed the tear running down her face.

The phone rang, and it was Coby calling from his hotel room. He and Sadie talked for a few minutes and decided to meet downstairs for dinner. They also agreed that they would call it a night after dinner, so that they could start the next day off early. Sadie looked over her shoulder at Kalli, who nodded in agreement.

★★★

The next morning, Coby and Sadie snuck away for coffee and a croissant, which was part of their morning ritual back home. Sid knocked on Kalli's door, only to learn that the other couple had deserted them. Sid and Kalli would have been mad if they had missed them or made plans for earlier than nine o'clock, but it was only seven thirty, and neither Sid nor Kalli was an early riser.

Kalli said, "I think Sadie left around five thirty. I

didn't even flinch when she told me to go back to sleep." Sid just laughed, and she opened the door to let him in. He was wearing sweats and a T-shirt, which she assumed he had slept in. She was fully dressed, since she had not gone back to sleep after Sadie left.

Sid said, "I haven't planned anything for the group until around eleven. How do you feel about going downtown and looking around, even though there won't be much open? We could even get a bite to eat." Kalli decided to go along, for lack of a better option.

At Sadie's prompting, Coby had texted Sid, who now texted back with his and Kalli's morning plans. Sadie was a bit sad that they were not all together, but Coby assured her that it wasn't a bad idea for Sid and Kalli to spend some time together. As if that idea gave Sadie a new appreciation for the trip, she raised her eyebrows and smiled a weird grin.

Coby tilted his head and said, "It happens. I'm just surprised that it's Sid. Penelope had her suspicions, perhaps because Sid spends so much time at Kalli's condo." He was glad to see Sadie's face relax.

Sid thought it was a no-brainer to avoid the coffee shop with the longest line, but Kalli insisted. "So coffee it is," said Sid. He kept her close as he pushed his way through the door and into the long line of people. Kalli made small talk with the couple in front of them. Sid placed his hand on her shoulder again, but when she turned and gently removed it, he just slipped it into his pocket. They continued to make small talk until they got their food and coffee.

Kalli drank her coffee and ate her Gruyére cheese,

egg, bacon, tomato, and lettuce breakfast sandwich as they walked down the sidewalk lined with shops. She had another sandwich and a pastry in the bag, in case she got hungry later. Sid just sipped his coffee, having already downed a biscuit with egg, turkey, and gravy. Sid avoided cheese since he thought he might be lactose intolerant, though he hadn't been tested yet. As they walked, they talked about lots of things, but mostly about commitment.

The big clock in the middle of the street was at nine forty-five, and stores were opening their doors. Sid and Kalli passed boutique after boutique, which sparked her interest but not his. The jewelry stores were easy for them to ignore, but when they passed a boutique displaying bridal attire, Kalli asked Sid to go back.

The window showed off a white, silk gown, not quite an A-line, with white Italian lace. Kalli said, "That dress looks familiar. The back of it is amazing, it's open but with lace. I've seen it." She thought hard about the dress. The dress had a modest front with an overlay of the same lace. When Kalli saw her refection against the gown in the window, she gasped and exclaimed, "My dream in the hospital. It was so real. I was marrying you in that dress."

Sid's face turned pale, and he didn't know what to say. After a few minutes of silence, he asked sheepishly, "Did you want to see it?"

Horrified, Kalli glared at him as if she wished he was dead. Confused, she first shook her head but then she pondered the notion. The sign over the window said *Smith's Boutique and Bridal Shop.* It showcased in the window was the dress she had so clearly seen in her dream. A barrage of feelings from her dream of joy, love, happiness and respect swept over her. The dream she now remembered had been happy, but Kalli wasn't. She was stuck in her wheelchair and wanting so much more from her life.

Kalli's breathing became uneasy, and Sid could tell she was upset. He knelt down by her chair and put his hand on hers.

Kalli could not acknowledge him, but her spirit calmed. A gentle softness crept into her soul and spoke words that were not her own. "It's not your fault," she said, not looking up.

Then Sid knelt in front of her and asked, "Did you want to marry me? I mean I did not plan on asking you to marry me until I was sure you were sure, but if this is what you want."

Kalli withdrew her hand, mortified, so angry that she couldn't speak. Her only thought was, *How could you?*

Just then a miniature poodle walked around the wheelchair. The owner made a remark about sidewalk space as the proud poodle strutted onward. Normally Kalli would have given her the finger, but instead she rolled herself to the left, which threw Sid off balance. "I will never marry you, Sid. This is me now, and I don't want you. I'm going forward with my life, and you're not part of it. You will only hold me back. I'm so sorry." Relieved to be regaining her composure, Kalli resolved not to look at her reflection in the window. She started to roll past the boutique, but then she stopped.

Sid still held her gaze, but he didn't know what to say. He felt like someone had sucker punched him in the gut, but he managed to whisper, "But you are the one.

I thought …" His words were resolute, his eyes were piercing but humble. He wanted her to know the truth.

The chair was turned directly toward Sid. Kalli was sorry for him. *Fool*, she thought. The she paused and spoke without thinking in almost a whisper. "No, you will always be the one for me, no one else, just you." It was a resounding truth that over time had culminated. He had found a place in her life for which she could not account. Now once again she realized the dream did have narrative, but she would not think too much about it.

Sid rose from his knees, leaned into her wheelchair, held her and kissed her. She kissed him back. Sid could have easily said "I love you," but did not want to give her something else to contemplate.

The dress in the window would stay there for a little while until Kalli would later in the day put a down payment on it if she indeed liked it. Nothing on that trip compared with that very time for either of them. The play was top notch, and New York was one of the most fun places they could have hoped to visit.

Sadie was not disappointed with her increasing affection for both Coby and his sister Kalli, which was reciprocal. Kalli found a renewed gratefulness for her life. Events sped up for everyone, but not to the extent that anyone lost track of anyone else.

Kalli had the thought that she had been waiting on life only to find that things did not have to get better for her to be better. She could not believe what Sid had done and how effortless it was for him. She pondered whether somehow the hand of God had been in it. She realized that she not only admired Sid's strength and tenacity but greatly appreciated his friendship.

★★★

On the way home from the airport Kalli received a phone call from her dear sister Penny. "How was New York?" the conversation began. They talked about their lives and how complicated things can get and yet how simply God's truths can penetrate their minds, hearts, and events. Kalli was not fully on board with all of it, but she knew where she was going, since she talked a lot about biblical truths with the dear doctor.

Penny cut her sister off as soon as the subject switched to her ex-husband, Rick, of whom Kalli had become fond during her stay at the hospital. "So have you heard from the dear doctor?" asked Penny. Kalli said she had.

The Uber driver, Sam, pulled into Sid's driveway. Sid lived closest to the airport. Everyone would come in to refresh, and then he would drive everyone home or they would grab an Uber back. Kalli tried to hang up, but Penny insisted on knowing more about where the doctor was. "How would I know?" Kalli said. "I only talk to him on the phone. You're the one who goes and visits him." Her tone was defiant.

There was a long pause. "That's just it," Penny said. "I went by the office last week, but it was gone. The office 1B was no longer there. I mean, it had been there, but they must have renumbered that address, and his office was no longer there. I tried calling, but the number does not ring."

The door was open, and Sid was waiting to help Kalli

out of the car. "Sis, I don't know what to tell you," Kalli said. "He calls me on a regular basis. Our sessions haven't ended yet. Last we talked was a couple of days ago. I will let the dear doctor know you said hi and that you miss him. I am sure he will be in touch." She smiled at the hand that was extended before her. "Bye for now," she said, and hung up the phone.

About the Author

Julie Williams is an independent author. She is the mother of two boys and is currently an empty nester as both children are away at school. She graduated with a BA in psychology from George Mason University, which does come in handy. She enjoys life and is grateful for everyone and everything.

Printed in the United States
By Bookmasters